Booze at Breakfast

Booze at Breakfast

Catherine W. Scott

To order additional copies of this book, contact:
Xlibris LLC
1-888-795-4274
www.Xlibris.com
Orders@Xlibris.com
125970

"Beautiful portrayal of the generational nature of alcoholism from a writer with expertise in the therapeutic treatment of the disease, and wisdom gained from personal experience. She has been an insightful witness to the battle to overcome 'problem drinking'.

Ben S., member, AA

"It's the 30th anniversary of your death today, Dad. You've missed a lot of fun."

Barbara Scott Marx,
daughter of John Ainsworth Scott Jr.,
Oct. 2013

"Behind these juicy semi-fictional layers of a family story emerges a clear, compassionate voice of vast experience. An unforgettable and worthwhile read!"

Susan Galbraith,
former writing teacher,
East Jordan, Michigan

"Catherine Scott weaves her personal and professional experiences into this powerful story of spiritual growth in the face of the devastations of addiction."

Barbara Schlicht,
LCPC, Westminster, Maryland

"Catherine Scott, a veteran therapist and addictions counselor, has written an honest and gripping portrait of a family coping with - and ultimately transcending - alcoholism. Drawing on her own life experiences and a deep well of spiritual compassion, Scott's narrative rings true throughout. Her characters are people we all know, people we grew up with. Their struggles, small and large, are handled with care and dignity in the wonderfully heartfelt story."

Julie L. Ramsey, Ed.D.,
vice president for college life and Dean of Students,
Gettysburg College, Gettysburg, PA.

"Catherine beautifully and powerfully expresses the main principles of the programs of AA and Al-Anon in such a way that I can see how living by these principles could be life-changing. These characters' pain became my pain, and, gratefully, their joy became my joy."

Hilarie Anderson,
vast and well-qualified proof reader

CONTENTS

ACKNOWLEDGEMENT

I wish to acknowledge Max Regan, Hollowdeck Press, Boulder, Colorado for wise, skillful coaching in writing.
- Countless encouraging sharings in Al-Anon and AA in Colorado, Pennsylvania, and Maryland
- writing support from my writers' group including Frances Jenner, Katherine Hahn, and Karen Mehringer
- copy editing by Jody Berman, Berman Edits, Boulder, CO
- and lots of encouragement from family and friends, especially Judy O'Brien, Leslie Varela and Justin Streeter, Betty Fribbance, and Robyn, Ethel and Hil.
-Amy Scott at Xlibris has helped polish the final editing.

A book takes a village, indeed.

To my brother Johnny—

John Ainsworth Scott Jr.

1939 - 1983

a bright lovely spirit who lives on in this work
and God knows where else.

Here's to you, J-bird.

You are the inspiration and guide for this work.

Johnny

1

Anika—1946

A five-year-old girl sat crying on the front stoop of a brick house shaded by a spring-green maple tree. Sobbing, she hugged her knees as tears trickled down her cheeks. Through her thin blue jeans, she felt the cold stone stoop hard on her bottom.

A chickadee sang its morning *chick-a-dee-dee-dee* call from a branch above. The little girl's wavy chestnut hair framed her round face and blue eyes. In her jeans, red flannel shirt, and sneakers, she looked the tomboy.

The child's kindly Irish neighbor lady, Marymoll O'Reilly, approached her young friend as she passed by.

"Oh dear, Anika-child. Whatever could be breakin' your precious little heart so?" She lifted a hand toward the girl, her brow darkening.

Anika sat up, wiping her eyes, ashamed to be seen weeping.

"Oh, I'm okay, Miz Marymoll. It's just that . . . he . . . he's so mean . . ." She burst out sobbing again.

The corners of Marymoll's mouth lowered. She drew her fingertips to her lips, watching. Marymoll O'Reilly had known the pains of childhood. Food ran scarce in Ireland, so her family had migrated to America in 1897. She had witnessed real suffering, heard neighborhood children wailing in cold wet hunger. She never forgot that sound.

She climbed the step to sit beside the child, taking Anika's shaking body into her lap, rocking her in gentle rhythm. "What c'n be so terribly wrong, dearest gurrl? Talk t' me." Black curly hair in a bun, green eyes alight with compassion, she wore her usual black rayon dress with the large crimson roses

13

all over, a black calf-length wool coat, open to the warm morning, and her signature high-top black sneakers to help balance her on bowed legs.

Her tenderness prompted a fresh burst of tears from Anika who burrowed deeper into the woman's lap. Marymoll held her and rocked gently.

Suddenly, the front door opened. Anika was startled, jerking up. She let out her breath when she saw it was her mother, Sally. She watched her mother's face.

Sally Mendoza was a pretty woman with green eyes and sun-streaked brunette hair. She wore a blue plaid cotton shirt and jeans. Looking down on the child and her neighbor, she wiped her hands on her apron. "We won't be needing your help today, Miz Marymoll. But thank you, I know you mean well. Come inside, Anika." She held the heavy wooden door for her daughter.

Anika swiped at her eyes and rubbed her hands on her jeans. Her shoulders slumped. She looked into Miz Marymoll's kind face once more. "Bye, Miz Marymoll." She lowered her eyes and went into the house.

"I—I didn't mean to bawtha anyone." With effort, Marymoll stood and smiled her compassion for Sally, but Sally's back was already turned as she hurried the child inside.

Somethin' very wrong is goin' on in there, she thought to herself as she headed home. *Dad drinkin' mebbe. Dear Gawd*, she prayed, *please watch over this troubled family and take Yer own great good care of our precious little Anika. I know Ye're lovin' her more than I ever can. Put Yer own peace in all their fearful hearts and Yer big strong arms around their whole household, my sweet Lord. Thanks t' Ya, Beloved.*

In her mind's eye, Marymoll lifted Anika up into the light as she hobbled along, holding the child safe in the hell that was sure to come. She knew Anika had broken the code of the troubled family: *Don't tell what goes on within these walls. Or else.*

Inside the house, the child hung her head in shame beneath her mother's glare. Sally knelt on one knee to bring her face close to Anika's. She whispered fiercely, her mouth twisting awkwardly around her words. "You took our family business out on the street?"

Anika saw raw fear in her mother's eyes, and it dawned on her that her mother was afraid, not angry at her. "I'm sorry, Mommy," she whispered, touching Sally's face. "I won't do it again." She let a tear slide out, beginning to understand in a new way.

"I've warned you about that, honey," Sally added, softening slightly as she saw that Anika understood the gravity of it. "You could cause big trouble, even . . . get you kids . . . taken." She choked and wiped her nose hastily on her sleeve. Taking a deep gasping breath, she glanced up the stairs at the closed bedroom door. She shook Anika's shoulders once gently for emphasis, then hugged the child close.

"Get to your room now and do something quiet—read a book or play with your babies—before you wake him up."

The sting of her mother's fearful warning clung to Anika's shoulders as she tiptoed up the stairs to her room. Though the humidity promised a muggy day, "a cooker" Miz Marymoll would call it, Anika felt a chill in her bones. She climbed up on her bed where her best ally, Biff, the gawky part Great Dane mutt, snored in his preferred pose, all fours in the air. She hugged him hard. He woke, licking her salty tears and slobbering his big spotted pink tongue all over her face.

She laughed. "You won't ever leave me, promise?" She nestled her wet face into his neck, liking the feel of his bristly short fur on her skin.

Anika's seven-year-old brother, Peter, heard her murmuring to Biff and sidled in, glancing apprehensively over his shoulder.

"What's up, squirt?" he whispered, eager for company. Their older sister, Cassandra, age ten, was off somewhere with her friends. Peter had been shooting paper-wad balls into his trash basket, listening vigilantly to every nuance of his father's fitful snoring and his mother's careful tiptoeing around.

There had been a particularly bad fight earlier that morning. Carlos had come reeling home, loudly demanding breakfast, 8:00 a.m. Sally had drowsily started the coffee and, as she set out his mug, spilled the last of the milk.

"GodDAMN it, you clumsy slut! Now I have to drink my coffee black," Carlos hollered. He heaved his bulk out of his chair and lurched for her, slapping her. She fell back on her spine on the counter edge and screamed as pain shot through her.

Peter awoke, listening intently, rage roiling around his heart. Someday he'd be big enough to protect his mother and give his father what he had coming. It would feel so good to smash up his face and kick him where it counted. *BAStard!* He hated his father with a pure rage. He pounded his fist into his pillow powerfully, repeatedly, his lips in a snarl, face flushed.

Then Peter heard, "Oh fer crissakes. You can't do anything right. You want somethin' to yell about? Go ahead, wake the neighbors." Carlos slapped Sally again, holding her in his iron grip so she wouldn't fall and break something.

Peter pulled his pillow over his head. He started to cry. *I hate that I'm helpless to **kill** him,* he thought.

Sally whimpered once, wiping the trickle of blood with the back of her hand, watching Carlos, knowing better than to say anything to rile him into the fresh attack he was spoiling for. She clamped her mouth shut, ground her teeth, and set about making scrambled eggs and toast.

A bitter tear pushed out. She swiped at it. She had come to fear and hate Carlos, hate the hell their life had become. Mostly she feared what it was doing to her kids. Her father had been a down and dirty drunk; now here she was in similar squalor, living her mother's hell, wanting more than anything to give her children a better life than she had had.

Defeat slumped her shoulders, draining her body of energy. How had it come to this? She had sworn she'd *never* choose like her mother, stuck with a rotten drunk who walked out of their lives when she was twelve. She would be smarter than that. *But I never saw it coming,* she thought, *and now I can't leave even to protect the kids. How could I support them without his paycheck? And he knows it and plays it. Is this my life sentence for sneaking out that night to go to that lousy dance? Is there some destiny holding me in its death grip, playing my life out in its dark measure?*

Carlos finished breakfast and rolled up the stairs to sleep it off. Nobody heard Anika sneak down the stairs and out the door. Sally was cleaning up breakfast when she heard the child sobbing and went looking for her.

2

Romance

Early next morning, Sally poured a cup of coffee and sat at her kitchen table, musing on her first sight of Carlos some twelve years back. Leaning against the wall of the Albany armory dance floor, brown eyes locked on her, Carlos wore an appreciative little smile. His skin was olive, his hair black. Sally thought him sharply handsome in his army uniform, crisp and spit-shined. "Entertain Our Troops Dance, Your Patriotic Duty" was the dance billing that had drawn her there—that and some hunch in her mind. This was a first for her.

A powerful thrill shot through her when he finally asked her to dance. She was glad she'd chosen her blue-and-purple flowered dress that flared when she spun and made her sandy blonde ponytail shine bright. They seemed to fit together in both the slow and fast dances and even faked their way through a breathless rumba. They stayed on the floor for every number until the band played "Good Night, Irene" and left the dance hall together.

"May I take you home, pretty Sally?" he asked gallantly, slightly Spanish.

"I'd love that, soldier-boy," she said. *What a gentleman*, she smiled to herself. He helped her on with her jacket, squeezing her shoulders affectionately.

They rode the trolley, necking unabashedly in front of the few late-night passengers and steaming up the window as the trolley car clacked along its rails.

"So tell me, Carlos, where are you from?" She snuggled into him on the double seat, his arm around her tight.

"Deep in Me-hee-co—Mayan co'ntry," he drawled to amuse her. "We were corn farmers, and Pop had a mechanics shop with a little grocery."

Good close-to-the-land people, she fantasized. She turned toward him on the seat.

"But you're an American citizen, right? You're in the army." Sally stared at his handsome face, wondering if he was for real or if she just dreamed him up. She touched his cheek wonderingly with one finger to be sure.

He smiled at her touch, understanding its meaning. "Oh, sure, I've lived here since I was five. We came as migrants with my uncle, and we stayed for the work. I got my citizenship when I was eighteen and joined the army to see the world, learn a trade, serve my country, and maybe do a little better than Poppy's garage work." He winked at her, clicking his lips. Sally liked the Spanish flair.

"Sure am glad I came out tonight. I wasn't going to, but something pushed me out the door," he said, blushing slightly. He brushed a piece of lint off the shoulder of his uniform.

"Me too! My mom would kill me if she knew I was out. But something told me I just had to . . ." She glanced at him, looking to see how he'd take her guilty confession.

He raised his eyebrows, pulling her close. He brushed her nose softly with his. She thought herself lucky to have such a hunk choose her out of all the others. He knew what he wanted and how to work to make it happen. He was a man, not like the boys at school. Brave. Patriotic, even—a man of the world. She felt a bit young in contrast.

She had known a Spanish girl in sixth grade, a snapping-eyed beauty named Suanie. What gentle ways, Sally thought, and such devotion to her family. One day she played at Suanie's house and saw the kindness of the grandmother and mother. They lived so differently than her family. Sally's mother had little time for her children because she was always working. And her father hadn't approved of Latinos or Irishers. "Goddamned spics and micks wanta take all our jobs and make our kids starve to death," she'd heard him tell her mother. "Oughta go back t' their tacos and taters."

Her father's bigotry flamed her desire for Carlos. She imagined hooking up with a Spanish hunk *and* getting even with her dad who left them in the lurch. The rebel in her rejoiced.

They got off at Western Avenue and walked to West Street and the little house where she'd grown up. She was glad her mother would be sleeping soundly, working all the time to provide for three kids.

Sally reached up for one last lingering kiss at her front door. His tongue played with hers, then explored her mouth. An exquisite fire burned in her belly and in her loins. She wanted more, lots more of this guy. "Um, Carlos, how old are you, if you don't mind me asking?"

Carlos pulled back slightly. "I'm nineteen. Too old for you?"

"I'm almost eighteen. Too young for you?" She smoothed his lapels.

"That's just right. I don't know what it is about you, Sally, but I . . . I never . . . man! Sangre de Christo . . ."

She leaned back, holding his arms, looking deeply into his eyes. She'd never felt like this before. Could this be the man she'd marry? They made plans to get ice cream the next night and said good night.

The moon lit shadows in her room as she undressed dreamily. She flipped on the desk lamp and tried to study her French verbs for her test the next day but could barely concentrate. She climbed into bed and fell right to sleep. She dreamed of eloping with Carlos, living in a cabin at the edge of the Mexican shore, lots of beautiful kids, some chickens, maybe a pig. Mangoes for breakfast, music always, husband coming home from work to be with his family, the happy intact family she'd dreamed of.

The next day as she walked the hall at school, nodding at some passing kids, she told her best friend, Polly, "I met a dreamboat of a guy at the armory dance, Pol." Polly's eyes widened. "Wish you could have seen him."

"I couldn't sneak out. My mother watches everything." Polly stopped to tie her shoe, making a boy behind her trip and nearly drop his books on her. "Oh, sorry," she said sheepishly, scrambling up.

"I don't know how you pull it off . . . and besides, I wouldn't cheat on Eddie. So what's this guy like? Tell me everything!" She smoothed her skirt as she stood up. Sally adjusted her friend's skewed collar and patted her shoulder affectionately.

"He's kind of a movie-star Spanish guy, dark and good-looking. Mysterious. And that uniform—ooh la la! He's got, you know, purpose, a future. Wants to see the world, fight for his country, and learn a trade. And I think he really likes me. He dances divinely. And kisses—ooh-wee! I can hardly think of anything else, Pol."

"Sally! You kissed him on your first date? Little fast, isn't it?" She saw Sally's look of shame and backed off. "Oh well, I guess it's done now. Anyway, Eddie'll be glad to have somebody to talk to. Hope he's a baseball fan too so Eddie has a sports buddy. I'm gettin' excited, Sal. This sounds like fu-u-nn!"

"If I can get out of the house again tonight, we're gonna get ice cream at the creamery. Want to come and meet him?"

"Yeah, maybe I can. I'll ask Eddie. Try for around seven after I wash up the dinner dishes."

Sally sighed her pleasure and squeezed Polly's hand. "It's good, yes, Pol? Sure hope you and Eddie like him. He's not like creepy Billy. I actually thought I loved that creep—you believe that? Remind me what I was thinking."

"You cut your teeth on that jerk without knowing why, hon. Seemed you were trying to find your father, like we've talked about. You're not likely to repeat that, not unless you ain't learned nothin' and you a particular fooool!" Polly stretched out her favorite word and rolled her eyes in showgirl fashion.

"Polly, you're the *best*. See ya tonight. Oh—how'd you do on the math quiz?"

"Aced it. I'm so smart." She laughed over her shoulder and strutted down the hall, wiggling her hips and swishing her skirt. She looked back with a wicked grin.

Sally's eyes flew open wide, hand over her mouth to stifle her laugh. She tried to hold her thrall in check so she didn't skip down the hall like the childish *fooool* Polly loved to make fun of. After all, senior girls were to act like ladies in their skirts and ribbons. And she had French verbs to think about.

Carlos reported for active duty a month later. Because he was bilingual, he was sent to Mexico to protect American interests in the insurrection against the Mexican president, Pascual Ortiz Rubio. He decided to wait until his next leave to ask Sally to marry him, hinting broadly in his letters. In August of 1932, he returned to the States for a three-week furlough. He had acquired a tic in his right eye and a drinking habit, which Sally attributed to army stress, explaining it away to her mother as "war heebie-jeebies, Ma, not like Dad's drinking for no reason. If you knew what he saw there . . ."

Her mother held her tongue and worried. She knew about heavy drinking, that it always led to some variation of hell. Drinking was drinking, whatever the excuse, she knew. But a young woman in love was a wild filly. Her words would just inflame her daughter, driving her into Carlos's arms faster. And what kind of example was she? So she sat at her kitchen table in late night silence and lit votive candles to the Blessed Mother, crossing herself, cursing booze for what it had done to her dreams, praying it would be different for Sally, her eldest, her girl.

3

Marymoll

Marymoll O'Reilly arrived in the world with curly raven hair and big eyes that stared straight into the eyes of the other. True beauty shone in the face of this babe. Her eyes turned a lovely green with gold flecks in her first month.

The six-month-old infant stared at the crusty old Irish priest as he tenderly held her above the baptismal font. He palmed a few drops to warm them, then drizzled them over the little head.

"I baptize thee in the name o' the Fatherr, the Sonnn, and the Holy Ghost. There. Ye're in, little gurrl," he whispered in muted baritone brogue. He held her up to his cheek, lingering in the delight, the soft smell and sounds of her. The infant made little gurgling sounds.

"Sure'n this one . . . specially anointed." The priest nodded to the baby's mother, Molly. "Those eyes . . . you watch carefully, Molly O'Reilly. She has the light o' Christ in 'er, so." He shook his gray head in wonder, eyes crinkling, ever amazed by new creation. He saw God especially in the thin places, the wonder at birth and death.

Molly's parents, Mick and Tilly, looked on smiling. The priest gave the mother her baby, carefully cradling the tiny head, tears of awe brightening his eyes. He wiped them away, saying, "I'm tellin' ye, that's a rare light in this one, Molly. Keep watch, eh? I'll be prayin', will I." He winked at Molly's parents. "How'd such a beauty be comin' from the likes o' you anyhow, Mick? Speakin' o' miracles, so."

Mick chuckled at the joshing he loved. "Seein' what yerself missed out on, ye mean, wi' yer own mug that only a mother c'ud love, so," Mick taunted.

Molly leaned with her child into her parents' embrace. A deep low wail came up from her belly, a mix of wonder at her beautiful child and grief for her husband, Johnny. She let it out, then just as quickly lifted her head in fierce Irish pride. Molly had been sustained by Mick and Tilly's love since her fisher husband's boat went down in a storm shortly before Marymoll was born.

"I thank Himself for this little rose o' beauty, Father," she cried. "She's all that's left o' Johnny O'Reilly, God rest 'is ornery soul at the bottom o' the sea."

Molly's mother and father looked on their daughter with proud love, glad to see she was resolved to make it. They would all make it together.

~ ~ ~

Marymoll grew into the lovely girl with the rich soul envisioned by the old priest as he had baptized her. She was named rightly, Tilly thought. Dear Molly's and the Virgin Mary's names joined together in holy intent. Well-loved but not spoiled, she seemed to have been born with a giving nature and an angelic heart. She reminded Tilly of the child's father, Johnny O'Reilly, with his own heart of gold. Lost at sea, he was jolly and sweet, not a mean bone in his body that she ever saw.

Molly asked her mother, "Mum, whaddya think, is this little one ornery Johnny's soul in a sweet gurl's body? It's improved, if t'is." She chuckled at the memory of his clever, pranking ways. "Always messin' with somebody, makin' 'em loff," she remembered.

"Sure'n he's funnin' with ol' King Neptune as we speak, darlin'!" her mother said with an eye-crinkling laugh. Tilly had loved Johnny like a son, having picked him out for her daughter and then engineered the match. She first saw him carrying his mother's groceries and laughing with her about everything they saw along their way.

"Did ye see that hat wi' the feathers on Miz Maguire?" Johnny said loudly to his mom. "Got it outa her ma's grave, and that's a fact. I remember so. Yah, Miz Maguire?" Johnny joked.

"Go on wi' ye, Johnny O'Reilly." Miz Maguire laughed. "Ye ain't had a day's luck in yer whole life! Think you'll ever amount ta anythin'?" she teased back.

Tilly set her sights on Johnny for her precious Molly-girl and started asking around about him that day. He was as good as married once she set her cap on him. Always kindly yet strong, Tilly had a way of getting what she intended. Few ever thought of saying no to her.

She got the word out that she'd like him to come around with his catch of the day at six o'clock one night when the family was at supper. She began setting a place for him each night "jest in case," she told Molly, planting the seed of welcome into the family.

Soon one fine night, he obliged. He stood in the doorway in muddy boots, his eyes riveted on Molly, and stammered, "Uh, I come by like ye said, Miz Tilly. Got some fish fer ye t' look at." He never took his eyes off Molly.

Molly looked down at her plate. She knew of him, that he was a good worker and a cutup, well liked. She smiled shyly, then dove into her stew, blushing.

Tilly noted her daughter's awkwardness. "Molly, dear, would ye be good enough to pick out enough fish fer tomorrow's supper then?"

Molly turned scarlet, a hint that gave Johnny some hope, and went to inspect his fish, eyes on the floor. She pointed to a red snapper and asked, "How much d'ye need fer this one, then?" She twisted her hands around each other.

"Fer yew, m' lady, it's nuthin'." He smiled tenderly at her, his heart pounding like a drum so loud she surely had to hear it.

"Well, thank ye, then, I'm sure." She flushed, curtsied a tiny flourish, and hurried back to her safe chair. Strangely out of breath, she stared at her food, unsure of what to do next.

Molly's mother noticed the two blushing up a storm. She'd have them married off in a year. She'd talk him up to her daughter and find excuses to throw the two together. Johnny was a fisherman—that could be bad news. Yet what working man there wasn't? Tilly prayed that the Lord would keep feeding the flame. *"Tis a grand scheme Ye've given us here, Beloved,"* she said softly in her prayers in bed that night. Her heart soared.

Next day as she made Mick's lunch, she slid his tea toward him. "Mick! Y'er gonna have ye a son-in-law, and a good 'un 'e is, as fine as the Good Lord makes 'em!"

Mick shook his head at his scheming, dreaming wife. "Y'er gonna be the death o' me, woman." He kissed her arm tenderly as she put porridge down for him. "Ye'll always be me darlin' bride. Now who's this fella what dares t' come courtin' me fine gurrl?"

Tilly gave him a "who-d'ye-think-man?" look, saying nothing, lifting her head to beam understanding to him.

"Oh-h—that fella that come wi' the fish . . . oh ye're a slick one, Tilly-me-love. An' them two blushin' and fussin' so."

After Johnny died, Molly and the baby moved into her parents' flat on a back street in Dublin. Molly found work as a housekeeper while her mother kept lovely baby Marymoll. And Tilly's great pleasure it was. She doted on

Marymoll, teaching her the ABCs and numbers when she was just three, recognizing what a quick, curious mind the child had.

"Bright little sponge she is, Mick," Tilly said proudly. "She musta got Johnny's good brains, and that's a fact. Not that our Molly's any slouch. But that one had a sparkle o' quickness t' him that his little daughter caught."

Mick brought home rare treats for harsh times, sweets and ribbons, and once a tiny orphan kitten when he returned from the sea. The kitten's mother had found refuge in the cabin of Mick's ship to birth her babies. Marymoll fed it with an eyedropper Tilly fashioned from a doll's bottle.

Mick and Tilly knew Marymoll was a gift from God, a precious gift of renewal for their aging years. Tilly whispered in the dark of their bed. "And she loves the kitten ye brought 'er, like it's made o' gold. Such a lovin' heart, the child."

"What a joy in yer heart, dear." He smiled. "I know what she means t' ye. Yer love fills up this house, does it now. I love comin' home t' my three gurls. And it hurts t' listen to the neighbor kids' hungry wailin'. Them kids hardly have p'tata peels to eat. But somehow ye stretch our pay."

He rubbed her head the way she loved. She purred like the contented kitten. "Ye're a dear, me own Mick," Tilly would say.

Molly and Tilly took Marymoll to mass after supper on Fridays, the child's favorite day of the week. She loved walking between her two beloved mothers, holding their hands, walking to be with her God. It was all very simple for her. She felt a holy, wondrous presence in church.

Smiling at his three girls as they made ready to leave, Mick would say, "You ladies run along and lemme be, and pray fer me crusty old soul." He'd be asleep in his rocker with the kitten, Jakey, in his lap when they returned.

Marymoll would carefully climb onto Mick's knee opposite the kitten and pick up Jakey while waiting for her grandfather to wake. When he opened his eyes, she'd say, "I love ye, Poppy!" and kiss his cheek. "I prayed fer yer sore legs. They feelin' better?"

"Ye-up, m' gurl. They sure are better, so." And he'd tickle her cheek with his whiskers.

One moist day in July of 1896, Mick hobbled home on sea-sore legs with his last paycheck in hand. Fishing was finished for him and his old legs, his boss told him. "Find somethin' ye c'n sit down t' do, Mick." As there was no other work in Ireland, the family readied to move to America where Mick's brother Paddy wrote there was work.

4

Crossing

The day of departure finally arrived, a drizzly and cold fifteenth of September. A sizable crowd of friends with a few family members helped Mick and Tilly carry their belongings to the harbor amid much laughter and a whole lot of tears. Their passage was on an old but seaworthy craft. Mick had researched it and chosen a strong ship with a good safety record.

Some wore slickers in the drizzle, some just gray wool, all the covering they had. Molly and Marymoll had new hooded gray capes that Tilly fashioned from old coats in the church castaway box. Mick and Tilly wore several layers of sweaters and pants for the voyage they knew would be chilly.

The group made a raggedy lot as they walked the streets toward the wharf, laden with bundles. They joked and cried, and some prayed in their hearts. And the friends wouldn't have missed this goodbye for all the king's ransom. Some dear ones pitied Mick and Tilly, some envied them, and all knew they would miss each other sorely.

"I don't believe we're really goin', Molly," Tilly confided. "We're only kiddin', right? Sendin' somebody *else* away t' America? Tell me this is just a scary dream I'm havin'."

"C'mon, Ma, buck up. Y'er always the strong one, wi' yer goadin' us on, me and Da. Watch out, Marymoll, ye're a little too close to that water now, me luv." Molly grabbed the child's hand, pulling her fearless five-year-old to a safer level.

"Hey, Mick," an old friend hollered from the edge of the little crowd. "Will ye send me some o' that gold them New York streets are paved with so's I c'n fill these broken ol' teeth o' mine?"

"Yeah, Mattie-me-mate, I will." Mick laughed, but a sob choked in his throat and gave him away. He and Mattie came alongside each other, arms around each other's shoulders.

"Heya, Tilly," a lifelong friend called out. "Who's gonna make me current pie like ye do when y'er all the way in America? I need m' pie now, don'tcha know." Tears shone on the woman's cheeks. The gray day matched the mood of sad farewell and apprehension of the pending passage. Marymoll brightened their spirits with her excited skipping along the way to the harbor. "We're goin' t' A-MER-ica, Jakey," she sang to him in his bouncing makeshift suitcase crate. It was wrapped in twine with a handle just her size. Mick had helped her craft it.

"Do cats get seasick, Ma?" Molly asked Tilly, sympathizing with the rollicking crated kitten.

"Guess we'll find out, luv," Tilly said with a wry laugh.

As they boarded the ship, the family hugged each loved one goodbye. Everyone was snuffling now, dabbing at their eyes, hugging Tilly and Mick and Molly in one last gripping embrace. A few shillings got shoved in Mick's pocket, a few cookies and cheeses and notes stuck in their bundles. At the very last minute, the old priest who had baptized Marymoll rushed on board, patting Marymoll's head, then gripping Mick in a final squeeze. Mick blew his nose in his hanky and put his forehead to his friend's for a last embrace.

The ship's whistle blew. They cast off.

It was a hard crossing with meager food, cramped quarters, and forty-odd passengers sleeping on their goods below the deck. The passengers told their life stories and fables to help each other pass the time. One woman with a lovely soprano voice sang songs of the homeland for the children; a few others chimed in. The children played cat's cradle, tops, and dolls. Stella survived mostly intact, though she needed a good scrub from Tilly when they arrived in America.

Marymoll kept Jakey out of sight of the surly captain, springing the cat from its crate twice a day. Jakey mostly responded obediently. He'd do his business in a little corner of the boiler room where she'd spotted some wood ash. Then she'd carefully dump his leavings overboard. Molly told her what a responsible kitty-mom she was becoming. Marymoll beamed proudly up at her mom with an "of-course" nod.

~ ~ ~

After a few days at Uncle Paddy's in Brooklyn, Molly found them a flat nearby. It had a maple tree for shade and a little yard for Marymoll to have her tea parties with Tilly and Jakey, who bore the fuss of a doll's bonnet for such state occasions. Tilly would slip him a treat for his patience.

Mick found work in a boatyard, cutting and sanding planks to exacting specs. He performed his job sitting on a stool to ease his sea-weary legs. "Fine workmanship, Mick," the Iris boss told him. "Show these young-uns what work is, will ye? Nobody teaches young-uns to work anymore. Heads up, slackers. This ol' man's gonna take two o' yer jobs wi' one hand tied b'hind 'is back."

Mick loved the respect for his careful craftsmanship but modestly played it down for his young mates. His eyes crinkled and his cheeks flushed. "Go on wi' ye, boss." He laughed. "Just a dumb ol' no-account fisherman, I am, so."

Molly found housework through Uncle Paddy's connections and paid him back for their passage. After a few false starts, she eventually settled into full-time work as a housekeeper and nanny for a wealthy Scottish widower with a passel of freckled redheads. She loved their good-hearted, ornery ways. They even listened to her once in a while. Their father, Jock, felt her gentle, strong spirit and its effect on his household. A few months later, despite cautious fear of another loss in love, he noticed he was looking forward to seeing her each day, making excuses to talk with her and lingering longer than necessary.

"I think he likes me, Ma," she giggled to Tilly one night after Jock came home early, seeking her out and blushing. "Is it too short a mournin' time then, Ma, since Johnny O'Reilly's passin'? Am I wot they call a grass widow?"

Tilly hugged her tenderly in reply, then held her away, smiling. "I want only love fer ye, me kind daughter. Follow yer own heart, dear."

Tilly saw a right kind of love growing by the little signs of Molly's special care with her appearance, a glint in her eye, and a respectful tone when she spoke of Jock, which was often. His kids had been making bets as to when their father would wake up to what everyone already knew: he was smitten but good. Frankie, the eldest at sixteen, winked at Chrissy, fourteen, when Jock came home and casually asked, "Hey, kids, how was your day?" barely waiting for their replies. "Good! Anybody know where Molly is?"

"He's never gonna ask her, the old fool. I'm just gonna tell him to," Frankie the take-charge eldest told his sister.

"No, wait," Chrissy, the watcher, observed. "He's stayin' around mornings till she comes, did ye notice? Where he used t' leave her a note with instructions. Give him a little time. You know how hardheaded he is, and so crushed he was when Mama died. Let him figure it out on his own. It'll go better that way."

Frankie knew Chrissy's wisdom was bigger than his impatience, so he waited.

Molly overheard them and smiled to herself. She whirled the mop around the kitchen in a coquettish little waltz, singing to herself.

~   ~   ~

One fine May morning two months later, after the children had left for school, Jock surprised Molly with a huge bouquet of daisies and deep blue irises, holding them out to her, grinning a broad toothy smile, his eyes sparkling with love. She dropped her broom, which landed with a loud "thwack!" Her hands flew to her cheeks.

"Oh, Mister Jock, you mustn't," she cried, reddening. She dabbed her apron to her face to wipe the sweat off her crimson cheeks.

"Any chance ye'd ha'e me, then, luv?" he asked hopefully. He saw her surprised confusion. "No hurry, o' course, Molly dear. Take all the time ye need t' decide."

"Oh yes, sir . . . I think I could . . . uh . . . yes, Jock, sir, um . . ." she stammered.

Then she winked mischievously. "If only ye'd pick up yer underwear once in a while." She reached out a shy hand to him. He took it, gently drawing her into him. He tenderly kissed her brow, her eyes, her nose, her eager mouth. Her skin melted to his careful touch.

"N-noo, it's just—I'm surprised—but—yes. YES!"

She nodded vigorously, happy tears in her eyes. She knew it was what they all wanted, a natural joining of two partial families into one working whole. There was a raucous cheer from the children when Jock and Molly announced their plans over ice cream one day after school. Marymoll showed her approval by drawing a picture of the whole family around a table. Tilly and Mick refurbished an old Irish hope chest for the couple.

Several months later, when Jock's shipping company moved up the Hudson River toward new markets, he and Molly were married, and the new family moved together into a spacious home built by a Dutch merchant in Albany. Mick was finally able to retire.

Marymoll loved it in the big rambunctious family that adored her. She even shared her cat with Michael, the youngest, who teased Jakey when he thought Marymoll wasn't looking. She was. She'd chase him and do to him what he did to the cat. He took it. The others knew he was just trying to get her attention, get her to touch him.

"I got it comin," he'd whimper. "Durn girl's got eyes in the back o' her head, and herself lookin' so sweet all the time. Ouchee!"

Mick and Tilly had a large bedroom with a high ceiling and outside porch on the first floor. They chose off-white wallpaper with seascapes that reminded them of the homeland. Molly and Chrissy applied it for them. Jock honored them like they were his own, which eased him right into Molly's and Marymoll's hearts.

"I love how ye respect them, me folks," she said, taking his face in her hands as they were getting into bed one night. He cupped her breasts in his large hands. Desire sucked in her breath sharply. She was surprised how quickly she had come to cherish this second husband, and felt lucky to have had two good men.

"And if I tell 'em what a luscious vixen ye are in me bed, will they still respect ye in the marnin'?" he teased her. She laid back smiling, pulling him close, softly massaging his back, loving everything she knew about him, grateful she had a lifetime to know more.

~   ~   ~

When it was show-and-tell time at kindergarten, Marymoll drew a picture of her new family and proudly announced everyone's names like they were royalty, the most important people ever, including Jakey, the cat, and Stella, the doll. She transfixed her teacher and classmates with her infectious, loving tales. Every child thought of the one who, if they were lucky, loved them like that. Their teacher's eyes misted over as she looked around the room at each child, those whom she knew were loved like that, and those who were not so fortunate.

At age seven, Marymoll went to her new school with two brothers. She saw a bright new world open its treasures for her eyes and ears. She walked the six blocks to school in lively anticipation of what she might learn about this new morning, and again each afternoon as she returned from lunch at home with her grandparents. In school, there was plenty of paper to draw on, and scissors and glue. She made collages of ribbon and paper, cloth and construction paper. And the letters she knew from Tilly's tutoring formed themselves into stories she could now read to feed her imagination. And there were numbers, and friends, and some kind teachers.

She'd often play school with Jakey and Stella at home. "Pay attention, Jakey," she'd admonish him. "Look at this picture of the beyootiful meadow with all the butterflies and flowers. Can you imagine ye're there right now, sunnin' yer tummy?" Jakey and Stella looked wide-eyed and properly interested.

She had a box of crayons she'd been given by her mother for her sixth birthday. She loved fashioning little girl figures with curly hair and plaid bows or straw bonnets and braids. Or she'd draw little boys like Dresden dolls in shorts, chubby and redheaded and blue-eyed, fishing or catching beach balls or climbing trees. She drew her dreams, smiling because she knew these things were real, somewhere in the world.

"Tell us a story, Marymoll," Michael would call down the hall as he laid waiting for sleep. "Ye tell good ones. They gi' me good dreams, so they do."

5

Cassandra—1936

The only redhead in the family lineage, Cassandra came with a flaming tongue to match the hair. She was treated like the queen of the hop as the first living grandchild on both sides and her parents' pride and delight. "You're a legend in your own mind," her friends later teased her. Cassandra would flounce her hair jauntily. "Jealous!" she taunted them.

When Cass was born, both parents doted on her especially since Sally and Carlos had lost their firstborn, three-month-old Diana, to a mysterious crib death. That devastated them and the grandparents as well. Carlos's drinking escalated from that point forward. He binged for days around Baby Diana's birthday. "Why couldn't I have done *some*thin'?" he cried to Sally. "I feel so useless. Some *father* I'm turnin' into."

"Wasn't your fault, Carlos. It wasn't anybody's fault," Sally assured him.

Grannie Mendoza, Carlos's mother, showered Cassandra with affection, calling her "my princess" and fussing over her. A baby lover with too much free time and finally a little discretionary money, she drove Sally crazy by popping in daily with trinkets or tidbits until Carlos limited her visits to weekly two-hour house calls. "I know you mean well, Ma, but you gotta respect our privacy," he told her.

Cass basked in such privilege and came to expect the world to lie down before her. Sally did her best to keep Cassie grounded in reality, challenging her tantrums when life didn't go her way. When Peter arrived three years later, Cass picked and poked at him, hoping to make him disappear.

"He's a person too, Cassandra-my-love," Sally would say. "I won't let anybody hurt you, and I can't let you hurt Peter. He needs our love and protection, sweet little guy. See how he loves you? He watches everything you do."

Princess Cass didn't care for that brand of fair. She just wanted him gone, this pretender to her throne. When two years later baby Anika came onto the scene, Cassandra was thoroughly displeased. Scrawny screambox, she thought. Why'd they want a useless thing like that? She couldn't even play with it, that is, IF she even wanted to, which she definitely did not. She huffed to her room to seek comfort in something she could control—her dolls.

Carlos's parenting consisted of yelling to keep everyone in line, like his father had, which meant out of his way. "Oh fer chrissakes" was his favorite phrase, sputtered angrily. It worked for him. Everybody jumped. He thought that was exercising control, a man's prerogative, a Spanish cultural way. It also served as a twisted avenging of his own painful childhood, taking it out on his kids. So his self-hatred festered, fed by booze and bitterness.

Sally's response was to put her mind to keeping a quiet spirit, a full refrigerator, and a clean house to minimize his outbursts around the children. She became the peacemaker, understanding his pain, consoling the children. When it got too much, she said to him, "Do you see you're becoming like your father? See their fear of you? Is that what you want for *your* children, what you lived through?"

"Oh fer chrissakes." Then a stream of his mother-tongue Spanish cussing that he reserved for his up-against-the-wall rages. Spanish fly, Sally called it. Knowing she was onto him and having no comeback, more and more he would be off to the bar to pool his misery with other misunderstood unfortunates.

Sally knew about hard-drinking men. Her father was Carlos's mirror when he was still at home. Alcoholic, mean-tempered, and selfish, he had left the family impoverished when he took off. Her mother worked hard at two menial jobs to keep the family fed and housed. Sally was twelve when she took over running the house and caring for her two younger brothers. The fear that Carlos would up and *adios* one day, leaving her with the kids to hardscrabble as she had done, always hovered over her. Carlos knew and played on it, threatening her when he was feeling his meanest.

"I dunno why I stay here. Nobody cares how hard I work for thees ungrateful family," Carlos would say, knowing his own lie but refusing to accept it.

Sally knew there was nothing good coming out of that old conversation, so she held her tongue, closed her eyes, and dropped into her heart.

One night at dinner Cassandra, now age ten, took her stance of justice.

"Thanks, God, for Mom and all the love she provides us," she said slowly, blessing the meal and squeezing her mother's hand briefly. She shot what she hoped would look like an accusing glare at her father. Sally got it, nodding slightly to acknowledge Cass but not set Carlos off.

Cassie would be all right, Sally realized gratefully. She swiped at a leaking eye with her napkin. All three kids looked down at their plates, careful not to agitate their father.

Carlos muttered, "Oh fer chrissakes . . ." Alone in his darkness, he got up and left the table for the bar.

6

Sally—1945

Sally Mendoza isolated herself, fearing anyone might find out what was going on at home. Or Carlos might embarrass her by coming in drunk. Or her worst terror—the ones her nightmares were made of—Child Welfare making an investigation at a neighbor's request and taking the kids away, out of her screaming grip.

Sally's mother didn't come around unless invited since Carlos ran her off years ago, claiming she meddled in his family's business. Sally knew Miz Marymoll O'Reilly two doors down; she'd had coffee with her a year ago when Marymoll invited her in for cookies and coffee. Sally coped alone mostly, feeling like her mother's rerun, trapped and hopeless, ever determined to make it better for her kids. She prayed to the God of her childhood to stave off depression as she went about her daily chores.

One bright October day, she took four-year-old Anika to the church's Moms and Tots Time to find there was a new young assistant priest, Father Joe, with a booming Boston accent and thick black mane.

"Welcome to the parish, Father Joe," she approached him. Finding him easy to talk with, she lingered to get to know him a bit. Miz Marymoll, the kindly neighbor, was serving coffee.

"C'n I pour ye a cuppa my good strong Irish brew, Miz Sally? And a chocolate chip for the pretty little lass? Wot's yer name, dearie?"

Sally nodded, smiling her gratitude shyly. "Tell her, my name's Anika."

"Here then, me pretty Anika, help yerself, so," offering the cookie tray to Anika.

Anika took to Miz Marymoll right away. Sally smiled on them as Miz Marymoll leaned over to meet the child at eye level.

"Thank you, ma'am," Anika giggled, and took a big bite of her cookie. "Mmm-mmm. Can I have some milk, please?" Anika asked Miz Marymoll politely, wanting to connect more with the nice lady.

"What lovely manners ye have, me gurrl. You just c'mon back here and we'll find ye a glass. That okay, mum?"

Sally nodded gladly, recognizing genuine welcome.

The three new friends walked home together, chatting about everything. Anika put her little hand in Miz Marymoll's gnarly one. Sally thought she'd found a kindred spirit two doors down, to her delight. Anika's quick endorsement of Marymoll was the most reliable sign. *Did this one come from You, sir?* Sally asked silently, flicking her eyes skyward. *Please don't let Carlos mess this up. You—above all—know how badly we need a friend we can trust.*

One crisp November morning, Sally answered a knock on her door. It was the parish priest, Father Brian, stopping by with an altar cloth Sally had offered to mend. Anika played with her dolls near her mom.

"How's it going, my dear?" he asked with a warm smile. "And how is your doll baby feeling this morning, Miss Anika?" His face was ruddier than usual after his morning constitutional. He rubbed his hands briskly from the cold.

Anika giggled shyly. "She has a cold, so I'm giving her a warm bath," she announced.

Sally brought him coffee and cookies, sitting down at the kitchen table with him, glad for his timing. She had some big questions on her heart.

"Father Brian, can I ask you a question?" she asked timidly.

He nodded. "Of course, my child. Ask away." He raised his eyebrows over his coffee invitingly.

She dropped her voice to a whisper. "Father, where is God when little ones are being hurt and confused? Can't He help? Or doesn't He care?" Fearing she'd said too much, she dropped her eyes to her lap.

Father Brian caught the bitterness in her question. He put his cup down and spoke tenderly, reaching out to touch her hand lightly.

"We cannot know the mind of God, my beloved daughter. We must take it on faith that He's with us *and* those poor little ones as well. They *are* us. What's harder for me to fathom is that I'm told He's also with that abuser. That's a tough pill for me to swallow, but I see evidence that's pretty convincing. Sometimes they repent. Like one desperate father I knew who beat his son like his father had done, then got roaring drunk and came crying to confession with his terrible guilt."

He shifted on his chair. "'Was God not there?' I asked my spiritual director."

Father Brian wiped his mouth with his napkin, remembering. "She was a feisty old nun, Sister Helen," Father Brian remembered, smiling. "I loved her answer: 'God doesn't make exceptions, Brian,' she said in her sure way. 'He's an all-or-nothing same old God where we humans are concerned. Did He condemn Jesus's murderers? I'd offer to you, my good Father, that He was standing there holding his arm back from throwing a lightning bolt at that man.'" Father Brian leaned back in his chair and laughed heartily, clasping his hands in front of him.

Sally realized with a jolt that she'd given away what was going on at her house, even though that father couldn't be Carlos because he never went to confession, or church, period. He wasn't the man Father Brian was talking about, but he was the same breed of bully.

"Thank you, Father," she murmured, eyes on the mending in her lap.

Later that week, Father Brian sat with his associate, Father Joe, at dinner, talking over parish business. "Why don't you stop around to the Mendoza home one day, Joe," Father Brian said, rubbing his chin whiskers as he did when something was on his mind. "Seems like Sally could use a listening ear. Poor soul's got her hands full."

Father Joe nodded, making a mental note to find a time for that visit soon. "Got it, Father. Consider it done. Any special reason?"

"Mrs. Mendoza could use a little spiritual support, is all. I believe her husband Carlos"—he tipped his wrist back like he was taking a drink—"and she has a couple of kids who might be interested in your youth group." Father Brian swigged his coffee.

Father Joe nodded. The next day, he made an excuse of dropping off some youth group papers with Sally, timing it before the older kids came home from school so she might have time to sit with him in private.

"Mrs. Mendoza? Lady of the house?" He grinned and tipped his Celtics cap to her elaborately as she opened her front door. She smiled shyly, glad for his company. She was dressed in a blue striped shirt and jeans, hair in a French twist, curly tendrils wisping at her cheeks. A pretty woman, Father Joe remembered from their first meeting at church a few months earlier. *A smile that crinkles her green eyes, and a sadness that seems to come from her very bones*, he noted.

"May I show you a few things we want to do with the youth group? See if your kids might be interested in helping me get this thing jumpstarted?"

Though fearful that he might have been sent by Father Brian to snoop on their family yet desperate for some help, she opened the door and invited him in. He seemed kind, fun, real, just what was needed in the neighborhood and especially in Peter's life.

"You may," she said, smiling a little uneasily. "Please sit down, Father Joe. Can I get you some cookies and coffee?" She always kept homemade cookies on hand for the kids and their friends' after-school hunger ravages.

Sally sensed he might be able to offer some real support. Her kids' school was a mixed bag of judgment and support, depending on the teacher. She feared the school principal as an authority rather than compassionate sort.

Tentatively, she asked, "Can this conversation be private, Father?"

"First of all, ma'am, you can count on my word to keep your confidence. I wouldn't last a day in the priesthood if I couldn't manage that basic rule." He pulled in his chair and sat, looking her straight in the eye as he spoke. "I'm young but not as dumb as I look."

"Well okay, then," she said more confidently, pouring coffee for them. "Cream and sugar?"

"Sure, thanks, ma'am, cream and one sugar, Mrs. Mendoz—"

"Call me Sally so I don't think you're talking to my mother-in-law behind me." She laughed lightly, filling his coffee mug. He noticed a dark blotch below her right eye that she kept turned slightly away. He shuddered with sudden recognition.

"How're your kids liking church so far? And how's Cassandra doing? She came to youth group once or twice. Nice kid." Father Joe scraped the cookie crumbs into his hand and placed them carefully on the plate.

Sally smiled at him, opening a little more. "Seems the kids like *you* maybe more than church." She shifted in her chair, putting one ankle over the other.

"Probably because I'm one of them—just a kid myself," he snorted.

Sally liked his light-hearted humility. She brightened at the chance to talk of Cass. "Cassandra's doing fine—an easy child to raise, Father Joe. Her grades are good, she has good friends, and she tells me what's going on. Her dad is even pushing her be a nun, but I think that's just his wishful thinking. She's only going on nine." She shrugged and laughed a what-do-we-know laugh, then rose to refill his coffee and the cookie plate, which he was enjoying liberally.

"That's wonderful. You must be very proud of her." Father Joe sensed defensiveness in her words. *Tread carefully, Joe.* He noted she hadn't volunteered anything about Peter and Anika. He stirred his coffee, waiting, giving her time.

As if on cue, Anika trooped in, decked out in high heels and a shimmery black dress with pop-it pearls and a wide-brimmed feathered hat, smirking to her mother.

"Ain't *you* just the cat's meow!" Father Joe said, standing and whistling a catcall. "May I have this waltz, dahling?" And he offered his arms in dance pose, which she accepted, sensing his childlike spirit. Lifting her onto his feet, he whirled her around, both laughing uproariously. Anika danced her fill, then looked triumphantly at her mom, who was clapping for their performance. Anika curtsied with dignity and walked off in a theatrical strut, brushing her shoulder straps into place before peeking back around the corner, giggling.

Sally shook her head, smiling a "that girl" smile. Father Joe sat back down, panting, looking into Sally's relaxed face.

"What a fine mother you are! That's a happy, confident child," he acknowledged, running his fingers through his wild hair.

Sally noted his warm, encouraging grin as he helped himself to yet another of her soul food cookies. Dunking it in his coffee with gusto, he held it up in toast to its goodness and as a pledge of friendship to her.

"You keep feeding me these delightful cookies, I might have to stick around. Yee-umm." He licked his lips, hoping she sensed his sincere offer of friendship to her and her family.

She nodded. "Funny, Father Joe. I get such pleasure from watching you enjoy my cookies." She repositioned the clip holding her hair with both hands. "I love watching my family at the table, wolfing down my cooking. Feels like my gift of love, like I'm nourishing their souls or some highfalutin' thing." She threw back her head and released a high-pitched surprised laugh, embarrassed by her claim of high calling in ordinary tasks.

"Not so highfalutin as you may think, Miss Sally." Now he was looking intensely in her eyes, serious and speaking low, as though channeling wisdom from beyond himself, a kind of "now hear this" tone.

"It *is* high calling, Sally. God is in all our special gifts—and your cooking is a gift—showing us God's manifest self. Where else would these callings come from, and why else would they feel so meaningful to us? And you're especially gifted at it, which is the mark of grace working through you. Homemaking, cooking wonderfully, and nurturing that little princess and your other kids."

He pushed the crumbs around on the plate with his finger thoughtfully.

"You know how it looks when a fine runner runs, or what amazing sounds a great singer like Mario Lanza lets loose with an Italian aria? Or how a violin virtuoso picks up a fiddle and makes it sing? Or even when a great baseball player like Babe Ruth steps up to the plate, and you *know* somethin's gonna happen because it always does with him?" He took a sip of his lukewarm coffee before continuing.

"You've heard the biblical verse about 'a hand is not a foot, an eye is not an ear'?" he said. "Proverbs, maybe? I take that to mean we each have our province, each different, our little part in the big picture, which is God's kingdom. What if yours is cooking and homemaking to nurture precious bodies and souls? Is there anything more important? Especially to God who gave the gift of life to each of these little ones?"

She stared at this young man, feeling the stirring of a powerful new hope within her, alongside fear that she was being arrogant to see herself too grandly. Perhaps he *could* help her and the kids, she dared to think. *Give them a decent man to look up to and a friend and guide for me,* she mused. *Maybe, just maybe, this is the answer from God I've been praying for every time I take the kids to church.*

The door flew open. Sally jumped. Father Joe noticed, jerking his chin up with a little supportive smile. Cass stepped in with her two pals, laughing at a private joke on their gym teacher. She stopped in midsentence as she saw their visitor, a rarity in their home, and the priest at that.

"Father Joe! What're *you* doin' here?" She took in the comfortable feeling between her mother and the new assistant priest "Faith . . . Nancy," she said, turning to her friends, "this is Father Joe from our church. Father Joe, these are my friends, Faith and Nancy. See if you can talk them into comin' to youth group, and I'll come more often too. I need bench strength there." She grinned at him, pulling her jacket off, winging it at her hook and landing it expertly. "Two points! I'm go-ood."

Cass hoped this chance meeting might bring her worlds together a bit more—family, friends, church life. She took a step back, letting Father Joe work his charm on them.

"Well, m' ladies, and what could a man o' th' cloth be learnin' from you pretty things today?" He theatrically tipped an invisible top hat to Nancy and Faith. He talked the girls' language so his charm worked. The three girls began attending youth group regularly. Faith whispered to Cass at their first get-together, "Never knew church to be *fun* before. This guy is cool. We gotta bring everybody."

7

Peter—1948

Blue eyed and brunette, a comely lad of nine, Peter lived for basketball, and in his dreams of life as a Viking warrior. He'd written a "Heroes of History" profile in school with his buddy Spike for a class project. Now everyone at school called them the Viking Spies. The boys often climbed the maple tree in front of Peter's house which provided easy footholds, imagining themselves high in their pirate ship rigging, spying on the merchant ships that were easy booty for such clever, enterprising bravados.

"Ship ahoy, matey," growled Peter. "Git yer cutlass ready at yer side. This looks like a British cargo ship comin'."

"What's a cutlass?" said Spike in a stage whisper. "Some kind of bogus knife made to cut less? Heh-heh—I'm so funny. And how do you know all this stuff anyway?"

"Think it's a knife, a short curvy kind. Some Long John Silver weapon in *Treasure Island*, remember? Or didn't you get around to that book either?" Peter stage-whispered back, laughing to soften his judgmental tone, knowing he was considered the leader among his friends and not wanting to hurt Spike's feelings.

Spike just grinned and made a smirky face. "Yeah, smart guy. I read it." He grabbed a branch above him and pulled himself lightly astride it, making little butt adjustments against its hardness.

That morning, Carlos had sat at the breakfast table looking at Peter's report card. "Think you're too smart to listen in school, not fool around, and get a decent report card? Watch yourself, boy. I'm warnin' ya. I brought you into this world an' I c'n take you out any day, chico."

Sally flashed Peter a look that said, *Don't mind him, love.*

Carlos intercepted the look, mocking her in sing-song. "Mama's itty bitty baby bo-oy." He thought her way too soft on Peter.

Peter slid out of his seat, seething. "As and Bs are pretty darned good, Dad. It's just that one deportment grade that's a C for joking around. And those are a lot better than the other kids' grades."

Carlos grabbed his arm and hissed, "Get back here and finish that breakfast. You think food is to be wasted? Si' down." He shoved Peter into his seat. "I work hard for this grub, Mama's little prince-boy. You will eat it and be grateful you got food to eat."

Sally squared her shoulders and interceded quietly. "I'm proud of those grades, Carlos. He's doing fine in school, his teacher thinks."

Anika watched this familiar scene. A tear slid down her cheek. *Peter just has to walk in the room to make Dad mad,* she thought. *Unfair.*

"Hey, Pete, race ya to be president of the Clean Plate Club," she said, trying to distract her father. Peter shot her a guarded, grateful look. Brother and sister were allies in this nightmare. They dove into their dinners.

Peter's dark secret that he told no one was that the bachelor neighbor, Jack Storrs, had been molesting him since he moved into the neighborhood two years ago. Peter delivered Jack's newspapers. Jack had slowly won Peter's trust by courting the boy with small favors and kindness and the show of interest in him. "Peter, wait 'til you see what I bought for you. C'mon, you're gonna love this." He threw a back room door open with a flourish. A snazzy electric train was all set up. "It's yours, Pete." Peter tried the switch. "Wow! This is just what I've wanted. Man." He raced it around and around. Jack came up behind him and stroked his head, his back, his shoulders.

Now it had become a regularly weekly tryst. Peter's disgust cut deeper every time he went back, but he didn't know how to get out of it. He acted increasingly surly toward Jack, to no effect.

Anika felt Peter's pain like it was her own. She would gladly have taken Carlos's wrath to spare Peter. *This stinks!* her heart screamed. So when Peter sneaked into her room early some mornings, she wakened and threw back the covers for him. They had a guilty secret, which they both felt as love and protection, though very wrong at the same time.

Anika thought she was championing and comforting Peter, though she felt deep shame in what they did. Perhaps her worst conflict was that it felt good though it was so wrong. Peter was motivated by lust, and by revenge against the tyranny of Carlos, and by the terrible conflict he carried about Jack Storrs. Somehow if he did it with Anika, it spread the pain around a bit. Guilt festered way down deep in his heart.

Peter thought his father's hatred was somehow his fault. What else could a child think? Carlos didn't treat anyone else with such venom. And Jack Storrs doubled his self-hatred. "Do you think I was born despicable, Annie?"

"How can you think that, Pete? You're so wonderful." She adored him. So they continued their shameful sneaking around. It left terrible scars on their hearts.

8

Anika—1949

On a bright June morning, a sparkler, eight-year-old Anika put on her sneakers which spelled walk time. Biff, perched on her bed, pricked up his ears in the hope he might score a walk. Two blocks south of Lark Street was the children's elementary school where Peter played pick-up ball every decent Saturday morning year-round. When Father Joe could, he joined them. The boys loved it when he came. It raised the games up a notch.

Eleven blocks west, a city park had a five-foot stream running through oak woods, Anika's special spot. She loved to sit on a large flat boulder and bask in the quiet, the birdsong, a peace like she felt nowhere else. She slid away and laid on her rock every chance she got, watching the undersides of the leaves, the changing shapes of clouds. There was a presence, a wondrous indefinable quality she felt here.

"It's so special, Miz Marymoll," she had told her friend wistfully, believing it was real important, though she had no words to describe it. Marymoll looked deep into her young friend's eyes, holding her shoulders. "I know just wot ye mean, baby. An' ye're that special an' important too. Gawd tol' me."

Peter, now ten, stood in her doorway, tossing his ever-present basketball from hand to hand. He was itching for the magic hour of 10:00 when his basketball buddies would show up at the court, having dispensed with their chores. His were done, and hanging around the house was not smart for him. Carlos could always find a fight to pick or at least another chore to assign.

"Where ya goin', kiddo?" Peter watched his ball so it didn't bounce.

"Going out to my rock, Pete. You playing ball this morning?" She patted Biff consolingly. "Sorry, buddy." He put his head between his paws dejectedly.

"Yeah, the guys and maybe Father Joe."

"Mom? I'm going to the park, okay?" she hollered downstairs to her mom, knowing Sally knew where to find her. "Want to come, Pete?" He nodded.

"Okay, hon. Be home for lunch please," Sally yelled up the stairs, knowing her 'rock time' was vital to Anika. "You going to practice, Pete?" Sally called up the stairs.

"First I'm goin' with Annie, okay Mom? Then practice. See ya'."

Anika grinned at him as they ran out of the house, Anika in the lead. Peter's ball bounced a rhythm as he caught up, hitting an easy stride alongside her. Anika smiled in their secret code of conspiracy against the tyranny of their father's house.

"Pete . . . uh, I'm glad . . . uh, thanks for comin'." Appreciation for his company and breathlessness made her stutter.

"Yeah, I know, squirt. Me too." He cuffed her shoulder affectionately. "Race ya'!" He took off sprinting.

They reached the park. She made a beeline for her rock and climbed on its warm welcome, leaving room for Peter. Lying on their backs, they smiled at each other as they soaked up the peace in silence. They watched for animal shapes in the clouds. The brook below offered up its cool dampness.

"See the fox, Pete? Or is it a dog? And over there—an alligator, see? Pretty cool," Anika whispered after a moment, hoping he was feeling the holy wonder, the great connection that she felt here.

"It's just a rock and sky and clouds like millions of others, Annie." He saw her wince and was immediately sorry but too stubborn to back down.

Anika bit her lip, looking away. She couldn't even trust *Peter* with her best thing. Why couldn't he get how important this was? Maybe she was just too weird—so weird that not even her brother, the closest to her, understood. Little wonder nobody paid her any mind then. She swiped at a tear she hoped he didn't notice.

Seeing, Peter rose up on his elbows and looked at his sister as if he was just now really seeing her. After a while he said, "Sorry, squirt. I get it now. Thanks for letting me in on this cool place."

Her dark blue eyes crinkled in a grin that she turned full face at him. She snuggled into him and muffled into his chest, "It's okay, Pedro. I knew you'd get it someday. This is where I—um—meet G-god. At least I think it's God. It's something out of this world. It's big, and it's kind, and so beautiful." She choked on her deep feelings, afraid to look at him, embarrassed to claim such big things.

Peter's eyes grew wide. He didn't know anyone who talked about God like this, as if He was her buddy, so personal and real. He felt a pang of envy as he stared at her. *Maybe it's just a girl thing. I better talk to Father Joe about this.* He stood up and stretched. "Best get going to practice. You gonna stay here awhile?"

"Yeah, I'm gonna lie here awhile. Too good to miss. See ya back at home then."

"So long, sis." He loped down the path, the ball hitting ground with dull thuds.

Anika wiggled into a little hollow that contoured perfectly as if made for her, sighing her pleasure luxuriously. "Hi, Goddie," she whispered. She closed her eyes and breathed deep, utterly at peace. She drifted off in a reverie of big warm arms holding her, cherishing her. The sun warmed her down to her bones. Anika smiled a joyful grin as a slight breeze fanned her face and neck.

"Thank you, Goddie. You're so good to me." And she slept a nourishing little nap as the brook slid by silently.

9

Father Joe

Growing up in Boston held many wonders for the young Joseph O'Rourke, who would become Father Joe. The Irish roots of his beloved pro-basketball team, the Celtics, reached back to the medieval Celts in the fourteenth century, which he discovered while researching Celtic spiritual beliefs. "Damn!" he exploded in the quiet library upon that discovery. He loved the images of joyful Celtic dancing in the wee hours on the moors, reveling in God's rich colorful sensuality. Such outrageous fun was often forbidden in the church, so it delighted his soul to dance and spin like a Celt as he plied his natural gifts on the basketball court.

At heart, Joe was a fun-seeker, a romantic, an epicure, character traits he well knew to keep under wraps around his religious superiors. He called this aspect of himself "Sunny, the Dancing Fool." Because he had to hold this part close to his chest, he felt it as his secret space for God, the most sacred gift he held for God. He couldn't remember a time before he knew that God was real in his heart. As his spiritual growth matured, he realized that Sunny *was* the dancing God within him.

"*God, You are so bloomin' awesome, in all beautiful and wonder-full things,*" he prayed in private. "*You are the ocean, the flowers, the seagulls. Don't let our secret out, and I sure won't. They'd lock me up for heresy for sure. Ain't no catechism for all that natural wonder.*"

And Joe loved the ocean. He spent as much time as he could there, walking along its edge in winter, exploring tidal pools in summer, swimming, sailing, or just gazing on its vastness.

Father Joe had a partner, Theo (Tay-o), a smart, kind, good-looking wine importer from Bordeaux in southwestern France. When the two met at a contemplative Catholic retreat on the Maryland shore in 1938, chemical attraction and minds meeting drew them together like magnets. They walked the shoreline, then stayed up all night talking. They had been best friends and lovers ever since. Knowing God had brought them together transcended any doctrinal admonitions in their hearts.

Both were gourmands in many rich senses. Now they had the joy of sharing all the little showings of Love's abundance, making it the sweeter by two. On a visit to Theo's family in Biarritz, France, Joe asked Theo, "Ever occur to you why your parents named you Theo, meaning God in Greek?"

"Oui—it has, and it gives my life the special richness of their faith. They love God like they love life. It's all one to them. So they love and embrace you. Remember how Maman hugged you so hard you could hardly breathe when she met you? You knew you were family, were *in*. That's how they live—in light."

Father Joe drove to Theo's in Boston every possible weekend, where they had big-city anonymity and lots to explore, and the ocean. "You lovely thing," Theo said one day, sliding a chocolate into Joe's mouth. "I love that God brought us together from such distance, you know? Biarritz to Boston?"

"You bet, love. I believe God created you for my delight, because He likes me *just* a little better than you." He let loose his outrageous guffaw, holding out his thumb and forefinger close together as measure. Theo tapped him on each cheek, smiling broadly.

Both men knew the pressures of hiding from the world's harshness as gay boys. Joe's rough-tough Irish clan bemoaned his artistic, spiritual pursuits, suspecting they indicated gay tendencies. His hard-drinking bar-owner father and four brothers made affectionate fun of his love of poetry and art. Nobody else better pick on him, though, for Joey was the youngest and the favorite. He *was* different; so they watched out for him. His fine features and winning smile didn't hurt his popularity any.

Everybody had a nickname in their neighborhood. Joe's was Brother Francis because of his gentle touch with animals. He once coaxed a terrified cat down off a ledge while several dogs, a squirrel, and some pigeons came around, watching. His brother Alec threatened to lick a bully who laughed about the tenderness of it. That day Joe earned his nickname throughout the neighborhood.

~   ~   ~

Father Brian knew Joe had a connection in Boston but discreetly didn't ask and assigned him as few duties on weekends as possible. *I don't want to pry if he doesn't want to tell me,* he decided. *He's a fabulous priest. I couldn't do half what God is doing for these kids through him. Simple prudence here. I'll just hang around some with the parish lads to be sure it's all on the up and up.* Father Joe sensed why his superior dropped by the basketball court randomly. He was grateful for his boss's discretion. *Some things are better left unsaid,* he knew.

Father Brian watched Peter for any signs of concern since they were together more than the other boys, playing a lot of hoops. He sensed Sally deeply appreciated Father Joe's friendship with her kids, which confirmed his trust. And Father Joe was thoughtful about playing fair with all the kids. "You're all equal losers in my book," he'd say, ruffling their hair. "What'd I ever do to torque God off and get stuck with the likes of you?"

Faith was simple for Father Joe in an everyday way of living. "Draw near to God, and God will draw near to you, Miss Sally," he would invite her with a grin. Some days he had communion with her with their coffee and cookies. "Don't squeak to Father Brian. That'd get his eyebrows jumpin' up and down like a yoyo for sure. You can tell Marymoll, though. She's one of us."

10

Sly

Ever since he was a small boy, Sly Starner remembered wanting his father to throw a baseball around with him. He often asked, "Please, Dad, can we play some catch when you get home from work?"

His father, Sly Sr., would reply, "Sure, son. Tonight when I get home." Occasionally he delivered, just often enough for Sly to get his hopes up.

Sly would daydream in school about the fun of spending time with his dad, just the two of them. *He'll toss the ball gently at first, testing me. I'll wing one straight at his glove, then catch his quick return ball in my sweet spot. Dad's eyes will light up with pride in me. Then we'll get in the zone and keep it up, fast and slow, high and low until Mom calls us in for dinner. Then he'll want to play every night and even start me on batting practice. He'll come to a game and get excited and then want to come to all my games. I see it all—oh baby. Someday he might even coach my team! He sure is good enough. Won't those guys be amazed!*

This night Sly Sr. came home from work looking angry and weary, so Sly waited, already expert at reading his dad's moods at age 6. He had to be. His dad's moods dominated the household.

"Get me a beer outa the fridge, eh, boy?"

Sly knew. No baseball tonight. He tried to soothe his dad by being charming.

"Rough day at the plant, Dad?" Sly Sr. barely nodded, forgetting he'd promised a ball toss, settling into his beer and newspaper without a thank-you to his son. Sly went out to throw the ball hard against the garage wall over and over until it got dark.

One day Sly Sr. walked in smiling and called out to his wife, "Essie! Lookit what I got." He thrust a pay stub in her weary face. "A goddamned RAISE. Do you believe them tight-fisted sons-a-bitches? A five-cent flippin' raise!" This was a real bonus at his plant where no unions were allowed in to bargain for fair wages.

Sly seized the day he'd been waiting for. "Pop, that's great. You wanna throw the ball around to celebrate your raise? Huh, Pop? Please?"

"C'mon, boy," he agreed, grinning. "I'll show ya' a thing or two." They played just as Sly had dreamed it for months. Sly Sr. was surprised by his son's catching ability, as the boy hoped. He got into it, throwing harder, trick spins and left field throws, stretching Sly's skills. He grinned proudly at his son, then sliced a fast ball that sizzled past Sly's ear.

"Ha! Gotcha."

Why does he always need to look better than me? Sly wondered. *I'm just a kid.* He puzzled over his father's big ego and tried to keep up. When Essie called them in for dinner, they clapped each other on the back, happy, bonded.

"Wanta play tomorrow, Pop?" Sly smiled up at his dad hopefully.

"You bet, son. You're a chip o' me own hot stuff. I'll getcha a better glove this weekend—you're gonna need it to keep up with me. Now that I'm finally making a living wage . . ."

The next day Sly Sr. came through the door and banged it shut. With eyebrows drawn together, lips tight, he grabbed at the fridge, cussing a steady sputter.

Sly went for the guilt hook cautiously, pulling at his ear, eyes on the floor. "Still wanna play catch like you said, Pop?" He carefully didn't use the stronger "like you promised."

"Get outa town, boy, he said, shaking his head. Not after the day I've had. Bastards! They wanna suck the life outa me AND work me till I drop dead for a measly 'nother five cents an hour. You wait, boy. It's a bitch out there. ESSIE! Where the hell's the beer around here?"

Sly slammed out to the garage to throw his baseball hard against the wall until it was dark. Again.

11

Carlos

One crisp autumn Sunday morning, Sally boiled eggs and toasted English muffins for her family, reflecting on her youngest, now seven. This bright girl-child was the one most mysterious to her. Of her three kids— Cassandra, popular and strong-willed, then Peter, gifted, comical, and angry, and Anika—this quiet one was the most distant. Her grades were mediocre. She didn't show interest in anything but horses, and that sport was out of their financial reach. She was getting by, keeping a low profile.

Sometimes Anika looked terrified when called out to speak. Other times, she was feisty. Sally tried to make time alone with her and invite her thoughts out in the open, but it rarely worked. Sally thought her daughter was too independent too young, as though she didn't trust anyone, that she was growing up too fast. But then, who *could* she trust in their nightmare home? To a point, she could trust Sally, but then Sally would cave in to Carlos, and Anika would visibly go into hiding. Or she'd trust Peter. They were always together. Except . . .

Sally's reverie was interrupted as Carlos slammed the back door and leaned into it as he knocked the mud off his hunting boots. The sound was anger. His usual.

"Foul freezing she-it. Like to freeze my ass off out there. And no, goddammit, don't be askin' your dumb blonde questions, I did NOT bag a friggin' deer. You happy? HEY?" he yelled into the kitchen. His English broke off as he let loose a string of Spanish fly, wrestling with his boots.

Carlos reeled into the kitchen in socks and skivvies with face flushed by cold and beer. Spotting his warm breakfast softened him a bit. He carried his rifle to the locked cupboard in the hall, taking the shells out and putting them in the box above the gun.

"Did the cabinet lock catch?" she asked.

"Yeah, it's safe." He sat, or fell, into his place at the table.

"Almos' got 'im between those big skeered eyeballs. But then I cocked me rifle, quiet as a mouse, an' he skittered off. Big sucker, maybe five points. Woulda fed us for a month, the way you c'n stretch meat. You're good at that, I'll give ya' that. Now where's me whiskey, woman? Can't a man warm 'is bones at 'is own kitchen table after huntin' for 'is family in the foul freezin' cold?

Sally blamed his alcohol with a deep, festering hate. She reached up to the cupboard where his whiskey flask was stashed, handing it to him as if it were a rattlesnake. She put a juice glass down beside his place a little too hard.

Anika slid into her chair and glared at her father. "At it again, Pop, hunh?" She cut him no slack, and he took it from her, which always baffled Sally. "Booze at breakfast?"

Nobody else got away with that. *Peter would've been flattened by now,* Sally admitted to herself. *Cassandra would be stuttering and fluttering around trying to please him. It's amazing how predictable he is, and everybody else's roles too,* she thought bitterly.

Anika was emboldened by contempt for Carlos and pity for her mom, Peter, and Cassandra. She saw her part in the family drama as challenging him because nobody else could or would. It was plain truth to her.

Sally reasoned that Carlos knew he deserved it, so he took it from the littlest one, the most innocent. She loved Anika's fearless spunk. She wished Anika would sing out like that in other ways. Sally made a mental note to talk with her, to commend her courage toward her father, and to encourage her to be bolder in the world.

"Just the way I like my eggs, Ma, thanks." Anika smiled to thank her mother for the steadiness she could count on. Like nothing was out of the ordinary. Drunken father at breakfast as daily bread. "Pass the jelly, please."

12

Peter—1949

It was in his tenth year that Peter finally stumbled over his rage. Sally had been watching for it for a long time, his whole life really. It was a collision course that would come down hard. He had held his pain behind a sullen mask around Carlos but was the family entertainer behind his father's back. He had a cast of imaginary characters that he would trot out for his mother and sisters' entertainment in his father's absence. The one he called Dickleton Tomato had a face and walk all his own that would keep Sally and Cass and Anika laughing for entire meals.

Sensitive and bright, he did well at everything he turned his attention to, be it drawing, basketball, even singing. Schoolwork came easily to him, but it was often poorly presented and boring, so his grades were beneath his ability. He played hoops every spare minute.

"Hey, Father Joe! Why you always pickin' on me?" Peter grinned as he rode up to his mentor and pulled up in a sharp sideways skid.

"Hey, trouble!" Father Joe laughed at Peter's cool bike moves. "What brand of trouble you bringing me today?"

Peter looked down at his shoes and got quiet, rubbing a skinned shin. Not knowing how to start this conversation, he waited. He'd had a fight with his father that morning, an ugly one. Why was it that Carlos always trashed him, never Cass or Anika? Peter wondered. Willing to risk the wrath of his damn-fool father's grounding, he had sneaked out his bedroom window, desperate to talk to Father Joe, who always seemed to show up when Peter needed him. Peter could grab his ball and ride to the basketball court, and pretty soon, Father Joe would simply appear. He seemed Peter's own guardian angel, this laughing, basketball-whiz priest.

Peter slipped as he shinnied down the vine, scraping his shin open. *GodDAMN it*! he screamed inside. He slammed onto his bike and rode furiously toward the basketball court, kicking viciously at a neighborhood German shepherd who always lunged at him as he streaked by. He didn't care who saw him do it at this raging moment. He just had to get away from the endless pain.

"'T'sup, kid?" Father Joe saw the fury in Peter's eyes and reached out to touch his shoulder. Peter ducked, then looked down, ashamed, knowing Father Joe's kind intention.

"I'm just gonna kill 'im. This is it." Peter bounced his bike up and down by the handlebars.

Father Joe sensed real trouble this time. Things had been coming to a head—no holding it back now. "Pete—"

Peter jumped back on his bike and raced home. He knew right where to strike—at Carlos's beloved Dodge sedan. Picking up a fist-sized rock, he hurled it at the windshield furiously.

Carlos, sleeping off a drunk, heard the glass shatter and came shrieking out of the house, lunging for Peter. He tripped on a broken seam of walkway and crash landed. His forehead took the beating, opening a bloody gash. He lay with his face on the pavement, cussing and kicking the ground.

Sally came running out, trying to comfort and quiet him. He pushed her away and vowed, "I gonna rip him apart. Thees time he's *dead*!" He raged on, holding his head, cussing at the blood. Sally finally eased him inside, out of the neighbors' view.

Peter knew he would not escape from this one. There would be serious hell to pay. He jumped on his bike and headed back to the basketball court where Father Joe was just getting on his bike. Peter raced up looking big-eyed, jumped off his bike and ran to Father Joe. The good priest reached out his arms for Peter, who sank into him for a long moment while he shook and gasped for air. "It's okay, Pete. It'll all work out, son. Let it out, Pete. Let it all out."

Father Joe held him, stroking his head and back, until Peter found his voice. Peter sputtered, "He's gonna k-k-kill me this time. I busted his precious car. I'm dead. I just couldn't t-take it anymore." Peter sobbed. Fear and rage churned in him. He gulped air between sobs.

The good priest shook his head sadly, pursing his lips, gripping Peter in his strong arms, remembering the conversation recently when Sally told him of Carlos's drinking and abusing Peter. "When he drinks, which is most days now, he needs a whipping boy, and if I don't block it quickly, Peter gets it. Or me. Never the girls. He just yells at them. He takes out his rage at his own drunken father on poor Pete."

"Father God, please be with all the Mendozas now . . . this isn't going to be pretty," he prayed aloud as he held Peter close, rocking from side to side. "Help me be Your hands and feet. You know this is my own nightmare wound with *my* drunken father. Keep me clear and fair, Father. I know this is for my healing too, that You're broad and long in your healing ways. Be with all the family and protect my boy here when his mom or I can't. Thank You. *Thank You, Father God.*"

Peter pulled back, looking at Father Joe, seeing him in a new light. He loved this good man more than ever for this honest sharing. Maybe he wasn't done for, he thought, if Father Joe had been through this too. Maybe he could find new hope.

~　　~　　~

"Hey, Spike-o, any chance I could sleep over tonight until the dust settles around here, so I live to see my next birthday? My old man's gonna be on the warpath big time. I busted his windshield with a rock."

"Sure, man. I want to see your ugly mug around some more, not have to come to your funeral. I'll ask my ma but I know she'll say yes. She has a way of knowing what's happening—sometimes I think she's got some kind of radar goin' for her. And she hates your old man, for sure." He reached out a hand to hold Peter's shoulder for a moment. "It'll work out, buddy."

Spike's mother called Sally, who agreed with great relief that Peter stay over at her place for a couple of days.

As Sally poured Carlos's coffee the next morning, she said matter-of-factly, "Carlos."

"Hmm-mm," he grunted in reply. He touched his forehead bandage, which reminded him of how badly he wanted to bust his own father's head open when his father drank and got mean.

Sally saw the gesture. She turned to face him. "How's your head, honey?"

Her choice of words surprised him. Did she still care about him, after all? Or was it just a habit, like she was talking to the kids? He looked up quickly to read her face. He hadn't heard that word from her in such a long time. It reminded him of their lost love, which he sorely missed. That one word said so much—could she still possibly mean it?

She brushed the question aside, bent on the task at hand. "Carlos, please hear me." She sat for a long moment, then flicked a feather off her bathrobe.

"What Peter did was wrong. No question. AND—you know you're harder on him than you've ever been on the girls."

Carlos waited in silence. *She don't scare as easy as she did before that faggot priest started comin' around here,* he thought.

Sally pushed into enemy camp, steady and clear, her purpose giving her a rudder through treacherous waters.

"Spike's mom has a heart of gold. I know her some. But I want Peter to come home. I miss our son." She knew that inside, this rift with Peter was tearing him up, though he'd roll in a hill of cow dung before admitting it.

Carlos rubbed his forehead in small circles to stimulate the blood circulation. His eyes were closed. "Goddamned boy is gonna work off that windshield money. Cost me 100 bucks t' repair th' goddamn thing. An' he's grounded for that outrageous report card. Where's this bullshit stop with that kid, huh? When does he straighten up? Reform school? Is that his next step?"

But inside he knew it was as much his fault as Peter's. He couldn't seem to rein in his tongue with the boy. He would vow to himself to do better by Peter than his father had done, but every time he'd fly off and lose it again. He knew he just waited for Peter to screw up so he could blast him. The walls between them had grown thick, right alongside his frustration with himself as the boy's father. So he drank it, and it festered, fooling no one but himself.

Sally surprised them both when she quietly spoke. "It stops when you face your own demons and quit drinking them. It's not working, have you noticed?" She was afraid he'd hit her, but she went for the plain truth anyway. He thought of smacking her, then thought better of it. Damned priest would see the marks and be all over him.

Peter came home that night after basketball practice. He slipped in the door as they were having dessert. No one ever spoke of his absence again. Sally served him up a huge slice of apple pie. "Hi, honey!"

Anika grinned broadly at him. "Hey, brud." She punched him lightly.

"Hey. How's tricks, kid?" Peter slid into his place at the table, head down.

Cassandra chimed in, "Hi, Pete. Hey, nice game last weekend. My friends said your jump shot has gotten really slick." She took a bite of pie, looking proudly at him, defying Carlos.

Sally dished up the vanilla ice cream on each piece of pie, extra for Carlos, who glanced up at her and smiled a little.

13

Anika—1947

On a rainy Saturday morning in November, Anika and her mother rode to the grocery store, a trip carefully orchestrated by Sally, as Carlos didn't release control of the family car often. Anika, now six, was grateful for time alone with her mother. She asked, "Mom, what was Grandpa Mendoza like?"

Sally cautioned herself to choose tender words and not vent her troubles on this undeserving child as her mother had done. "He was a hard worker, honey, a quiet man. He expressed his love for his family by providing. Those were hard times. It was a lot just to keep a roof over their heads."

"Did he drink too like Dad?" Anika always went straight for the truth, figuring she was best at deciding for herself what was what.

"Not so much as your dad, honey, just on holidays. He kept to himself, always working. But in all fairness, that was the way most men were back then. Not much in the way of family life. Women ran the families. My dad was the same way when he was there, silent behind his newspaper. 'Dad who?' we kids called him. I'm sorry to tell you your family was this way, hon, but I know you always want the truth. That's a good thing, baby. You're smart to figure things out yourself that way."

"Mom, that time when I was cryin' on the front stoop and Miz Marymoll came by? Why did you get so mad? Was I bad? Or were you scared?" Anika's little face was raised to her mother's in pure innocence. It touched Sally's heart. She stroked the child's cheek and chin.

"Oh, honey, you didn't deserve that. I'm so sorry. I was more scared than mad. I didn't want you to waken Daddy for more fighting. I was trying to keep the lid on so you and Peter didn't get hit, and that pesky Mrs. Pierce next door hear us all screaming and call the cops." Sally scanned that nightmare morning in her mind, looking for anything good she could tell Anika.

She pulled into the A & P parking lot, turning off the engine. She was quiet for a time. "If you kids ever got taken away from me . . ."

Anika watched her mother stare off in the distance and felt the genuineness of her love. She reached out her little hand to touch her mother's arm.

Sally startled a little, then smiled at Anika. "I want to tell you guys the straight story, what's real that you can count on. I don't think it's right to sugarcoat it for you. That way you can decide for yourselves what to do with it. I think I owe you that respect."

Sally remembered what she felt in the insanity of her own growing up. She wished her mother had told her the facts. But her mother had complained bitterly or suffered in silence, ever more depressed and sickly. So she was left to figure it out on her own *and* worry about her mother. At least, Sally had learned to give her kids the straight scoop so they could deal with life on its own terms.

Sally turned to look at Anika closely. "It's this way, baby. I'm gonna bust my butt to see to it that you kids have a better life than either your father or I did. That's my job"—she lifted Anika's little chin—"and I'm stickin' to it. Okay?"

"O-KAY, Mom," Anika said with gusto. "Can I get sugar wafers?"

As they pushed their cart around the aisles, Sally realized how powerful her determination was. It was a strong sense of purpose within her. She knew it was vital to fight for her kids, unlike her mother who did the best she knew, but caved in.

"Annie, about Daddy's drinking . . . it's not your fault in any way. It's got *nothing* to do with you, sweety. He was a good guy when he was young, before he started to drink so much. He was fun and handsome and patriotic about fighting for his country and hardworking. I really loved him, Annie. I want you guys to know that you were born in real love and very much wanted by both of us. Cherished, in fact."

"But, Mom, why doesn't he just stop? We never go anywhere as a family anymore. If he was nice before, doesn't he know he's mean now?"

"Good question, baby. I think he's on a roller coaster he doesn't know how to stop. Make any sense?"

Anika thought for a moment. "Mama, do you love Daddy now?"

"Anika, another good question, baby." Sally squeezed her and tweaked her little button nose.

"Sometimes I do, sometimes not. Sure don't like him when he abuses my kids." She'd have to find a way to stop the nightmare from ruining her children's lives, from trapping them the way she felt trapped. She remembered hiding under her bed when her father's drinking started. She knew where it led, every time. Somebody always got hurt.

She'd teach them that they always had choices. Now there was a thought. Did that include her, then?

Anika wondered why Carlos pushed everyone away when she sensed he longed for company, that he was a sad and lonely man. And she wondered how she sensed people's feelings that nobody named. She just knew. Years later, a counselor told her it was a kind of hypervigilance, an internal radar, that kids from alcoholic and dysfunctional families developed to survive. She told Miz Marymoll when she was twelve, "I've just always seen stuff that other people don't seem to see. It's confusing, Miz Marymoll. It seems important but—I never know how to say it, or if I should."

"That's wonderful, child. Ye're s' smart. Ye know t' listen for Gawd in your heart, my gurrl."

~   ~   ~

One January morning, Anika saw Carlos kneeling beside his bed. *Oh, God, he's praying to You. That mean he's open? Show me what to do to help him please. He's gotta be the most miserable man on the face of this earth.* She stood silently watching him.

She felt a little internal urge to kneel down beside him. She got down hesitantly, unsure if she was welcome. Carlos reached out a meaty hand and clamped it lovingly on her shoulder. They knelt there together for a long moment. Pretty soon, she sneaked a look over at him and saw his cheek was wet. She knew God had answered her prayer, and maybe his. He told her what to do in her own heart and now her father was crying happy tears. *Wow.*

She felt a warm radiance infuse her whole body. She knew in that wonderful moment that she had a special Friend, a *something* she could actually sense, like on her rock. Her heart broke open in wonder. She had glimpsed love, though she had no words big enough.

Later at breakfast, Carlos told Sally in a tender voice, "Something wonderful happened to me this morning. A little angel knelt beside me while I was praying." Carlos smiled fondly at his daughter, a light in his eyes that Anika had never seen.

Sally turned from the stove, hands in steeple pose. "Oh, baby!" she breathed to Anika. "You are *so* special." She hugged Anika tight and rubbed her little back passionately, smiling warmly to Carlos over Anika's shoulder.

"See what you've been missing?"

Carlos smiled into his coffee, stirring it slowly with his spoon. Anika stood in her mother's embrace, soaking it up, knowing she had stumbled on rare treasure. Carlos was softer for a couple of days. Peter noticed. He asked his dad at dinner, "Did you have a good day, Pop?"

Carlos looked straight at him as if for the first time. "Yes, son, I did. How about you?"

Peter smiled at him with a shy sweetness. "Yeah, Pop, I got an A on my math quiz. Hard one too."

"That's fine, son. That's real nice." Carlos smiled affectionately at Peter. Next night Carlos didn't show up for dinner.

"Should I set a place for him, Mom?" Anika asked as they gathered for dinner.

"Yes, go ahead, hon. I don't know where he is. But I can guess." She smiled to Anika. "It's okay." Her offer of acceptance of the way things were.

That night it was back to hell for Carlos. But Anika had seen beyond it. She had glimpsed a new earth.

14

Father Joe

It had been two years since Father Joe began serving as Father Brian's assistant. The two priests got along well, tending their relationship with respectful listening of each other. Both knew horror stories of other clergy who didn't get along whose parishes and even personal health were the worse for it. So there was the motivation, and two good hearts to do the work.

Father Brian sat on the parish verandah enjoying his morning coffee. He looked full-face up to the sky, laughing in the innocent joy of a child. He felt fortunate that he'd found and still loved his calling and that God had sent him such a fine assistant from whom he could learn a thing or two. Life was good despite its many tribulations. *Thanks be to God.*

The atmosphere of World War II held the United States in high tension. Everywhere, manpower shortages, food rationing, and women leaving children to go work in munitions manufacture were uprooting the balance of family life.

One bleak Sunday, Father Joe preached a lively, slightly radical homily titled "Faith as Call to Action" that torqued off some parishioners and spurred others on to fresh action. A few conservative tongues started wagging to Father Brian.

"What's this, Father? Politics from the pulpit?" one woman said, arching her eyebrows high at Father Brian. "Soothing biblical talk is what we're wanting from the pulpit, with all the war goings on," she tsked.

"My boy is passionate. Have a little patience with him, Mrs. Hogan. I'll have a word with him." Privately, he told Father Joe, "You go, boy. Shake 'em up, stretch their minds with the relevance of Jesus's teachings to their lives now. You're a bright one. You can explain better than I the transformative possibilities in these troubling times. Wish God had seen fit to give me your brains. That and my good looks—I'd be dangerous." They raised their wineglasses in laughing salute to their contrasting gifts.

Father Joe had led off in a quiet tone. "As you know, my friends, in the world theater Hitler's Germany and Mussolini's Italy have declared war on the U.S. And since 1941, we've been at war with the Japanese when they bombed Pearl Harbor. I don't have to tell you, we are in World War number TWO."

He shifted his stance and leaned into the microphone. "What do you imagine God is saying to his friend St. Peter about the world in war mode? Many American women have had to resort to working in munitions factories as Rosie the Riveter slogans summon them into the workforce. War rations are making everything scarce. Our heroic young men lie up their ages to enter the service in zealous patriotic passion. Many families we know have been rendered fatherless. Who's taking care of our beloved kids?" He was shouting now.

Dropping his voice low, he came back at them. "And what do you think our God thinks about this, my friends?" Father Joe sipped his water, clearing his throat.

He's just warming up, Father Brian thought proudly.

Now in a moderate tone, Father Joe rubbed one eyebrow, leaning slightly away from the podium. His timing and movements keep the people with him, Father Brian noted.

"Polio survivor Franklin Delano Roosevelt is in his third term as president, while his popular, wise wife, Eleanor, models courage and activist causes for women. You remember all too well when Wall Street crashed back in 1931, causing worldwide financial panic and joblessness. Her good example *still* is steadying the financial rudder."

He looked around slowly, reading the congregation's expressions. Encouraged by a few bright smiles, a few nods of understanding, he pressed forward.

"Drought has created the Dust Bowl that is uprooting whole families, drawing them west to California for farm labor. And India? Mahatma Gandhi has declared civil disobedience in defiance of British rule, with much popular support. British broadcasting is creating new access to literary drama, making owning a television a desirable thing, if only to keep up with world events."

Marymoll sat with Sally near the front. The elder woman was intrigued by this unaccustomed worldly talk, actual current events, in a homily. She leaned into Sally's ear and whispered, "He's sharp, Sally, d' you think? And maybe just a little theatrical to keep it interestin'?"

Sally grinned at her, whispering back, "*Very* sharp, Marymoll. It makes sense to show us God's take on our times to guide us. I like this a lot. It lifts me up."

"Yeah, fer sure. Father Joe sees God as involved in our *real* lives, not just some ol' bearded white guy in th' sky, always scoldin' us, so."

Father Joe looked out at the congregation, seeing Sally without Carlos by her side, and other troubled families, remembering all too vividly his brother Alec's battles with *his* bar-owner father. They would leave Joe trembling in his bunk as they drank and ranted on with their lusty old Ireland tales, laughing and arguing into the wee hours. It usually ended the same way, drunken fistfights and visits from the sheriff. One or both were carted away to sleep it off in the drunk tank for the night.

He knew nobody in the house—not mother, not one of his four brothers, slept as this drama played itself out in endless repetitions. On any given night, father and son were best drinking buddies or brawling enemies—a razor's edge split, love and hate. It could change on a dime. One minute, they'd be laughing, the next swinging. He'd cover his head with a pillow and wish they'd both hurry up and pass out.

It ended the only way it could short of violence. One humid spring night when Joe was thirteen, Alec came reeling home and threw his house key on the table. "I'm outa here, ye sorry son-of-a-bitchin' old sod! I got me a job prospectin' fer silver in th' Colorada mines, an' I ain't NEVER comin' back to this backwater dump." He slammed his bedroom door behind him.

"Good riddance, ye feckin' freeloader. GO," the old man growled. That was their goodbye. They never saw each other alive again.

This was about as happy an ending to this Irish drunken craziness as an ending could be, Joe knew. Next morning, he hugged his brother goodbye.

"I'm grateful you lived through the wild nights, Alec. Only you could get away with taking him on like you do. He respects you and your guts. He'll miss you bad, but he'll never say it. I'll miss you bad too, but I'll say it, for sure. Keep in touch, huh? I'll come visit if you send for me."

"Thanks, buddy," said Alec. "I love ye. Take care a' yerself. I'll send fer ye when I c'n put a little money back." He meant it.

Joe always wondered if this family pain hadn't been God's way of calling him to the priesthood. He suffered so for both of them as he lay in his bed listening helplessly through the long nights.

Alec's move left Joe with a room with a window, a desk for his books and cards collection, a closet. Best of all was his new privacy. He'd made do for years sharing a room with a messy brother, lying low, keeping his stuff tight in a corner.

Father Joe shook off the reverie, wondering how long he'd stood silent in the pulpit.

"Did I lose my place too long back there?" he asked Father Brian later in their offices.

"Not at all, Father. You just showed us your quiet heart. Kind of a taste of God's own quiet heart. You're a fine one, m' boy." He threw an arm around Joe's shoulder. "Little nip before lunch, to settle you? God Himself delivered us a quart of fine brandy that's calling out your name, lad."

15

Marymoll

Marymoll had watched the progress of Anika's life with great care and attention. She was gently there as Anika skinned her knees learning to roller skate and ride her bike, applying salve and Band-Aids and cookies and hugs. Anika felt closer to her than to her own grandmothers.

Anika often dropped in on Marymoll with her latest school project or an abandoned baby squirrel, or sometimes with the need for a hug and a kind word. She always left feeling filled up, both heart and tummy. She told Sally how nice Marymoll was. Sally marveled at their good fortune in having chanced such a kind neighbor. She often wondered what they would do without such friends as Father Joe and Miz Marymoll. Surely, someone was looking after them, and so graciously.

"I don't know how to thank you, Miz Marymoll—Anika adores you, has from day one," Sally said as Marymoll answered her knock on the door. "Here are some warm cookies for the kindest lady in the neighborhood. Maybe the whole city!"

"Can ye come in fer a cup of tea then?" Marymoll was grateful her loving intent was received as such by this worthy hard-times soul. Marymoll admired Sally. Her watchful eye saw the young woman's courage and tenacity. Sally felt profound love in Marymoll's presence.

"How are your knees holding up, dear one?" Sally asked Marymoll as she sat at the kitchen table, chin in palms. Marymoll's arthritis in knees and elbows were making it ever harder for her to walk or even stand for long. She never complained, but Sally saw the wince in her eyes as she stood or turned.

She was slower getting around. Sally's love for Marymoll grew in respect for her friend's courageous selflessness.

"Not too bad, m' dear. Oh 'n how wonderful t'is now t' have a chance t' visit with ye, as busy as ye are. I so 'preciate ye comin' by t' visit an ol' lady."

Sally had come to trust Marymoll completely and often sought her listening ear through the difficult years of Carlos's crazy rages. Marymoll never judged but listened with patience. "You're my role model, old dear," Sally told her. "I often think back to things you've said when I feel low. Gives me courage and new ways of seeing."

When Sally would process the latest episode of alcoholic insanity, Marymoll would say kindly, "You're all right—you're still breathin'." At first, that odd response struck Sally as a lack of understanding, or advising her to accept the unacceptable, or perhaps just disinterest. But in time, as she watched the loving care in Marymoll's face and began listening with open ears to her, she realized the wisdom in the words. Very gradually she began to let go of fear. She *was* all right; she *was* alive. And Peter, who often got the brunt of it, was surviving too.

Marymoll saw Sally's strength and spoke to it, and that gave Sally the courage to endure. She had, so she knew Sally would. So Sally gradually came to rely on her conversations with Marymoll, to think on them when she returned home. That alone helped her learn to trust herself, to look within for answers, and to comfort Peter with wisdom and strength. Their home grew calmer. Carlos stayed away more.

When later Sally started in Al-Anon, she came to see that Marymoll had acted as the perfect sponsor, a trusted confidante to whom she could turn for personal counsel, helping her sort out the good from the garbage, not judging her or Carlos, but simply listening, understanding that things were what they were.

She shared one night in Al-Anon years later: "At first I thought that Irishwoman was plain nuts, or just putting me off. But I asked her one time why she often responded with that approach, that I was all right because I was still breathing. She said, 'I didn't think pity'd help ye much. It never helped me think straight. Ye needed t' stay strong like ye are.'"

Thus it was that Sally had come to trust in what Al-Anon later called higher power, or the God of her understanding. It was not what she was taught in the church—the catechism, theology, penance for sins—all pretty dry and empty for her. She had known she was missing something important. Until now. In Marymoll and in Father Joe, she tasted love. They modeled that strong love so she could taste it, try it on.

One rainy day, she popped in on Marymoll. She was too excited to sit at the table. She stood with her hands in prayer position, tapping palms together. "It's the most amazing, WONderful thing, Miz Marymoll! I *feel* a powerful presence inside me! It's incredible—could that be God in me? Taking me above this troubling world into higher SOMEthing—the God of the whole universe working in me, healing me? You're the one who's shown this to me, my beloved friend, just by modeling it in your humble way. You—and . . ."

Sally paused and looked out the window. "Marymoll, I walked to Anika's rock and sat there yesterday. And everything lit up. It's as though the scales were peeled away from my eyes. Oh! Wild wonderful stuff, hunh? NOW I see how you are so sustained by your faith. It's so beautiful from His eyes."

Marymoll's hands lifted to her lips, overwhelmed with gratitude for this healing in her friend's soul. She swiped tears of joy, shaking her head in wonder. "I been prayin' fer this day. And ye know, dearest, I heard once that ye don't need t' worry about drunks, that God luvs His alcoholics and takes special care of them, which is why they seem to have nine lives . . ." except her man, Seamus, who choked on his own vomit and died in a gutter. *God luv him*, she thought. *A good man when he weren't drinkin'.*

Sally ran home to greet her kids after school. Marymoll sat and raised her eyes heavenward, smiling. *Thank Ye fer findin' me worthy t' use fer Yer hands 'n' feet. And thank ye, Mum an' Gran an' Ol'Da, fer teachin' me all th' good ye knew! Ye've given me sech a life o' wonderin' love! Kept me goin' when my Seamus died. Maybe fer this very day?*

She sat in her rocker and rubbed her sore knees and was content.

16

Father Joe—1946

"T'sup, sport?" was his every-kid greeting. He always had time for young ones—his "retreads and rejects," as he liked to call them, or "'ject" for short. He saw God smiling or crying in them all, his beloved young ones.

"Father Joe, you're gonna get us all fired for running the priesthood-of-too-much-fun," his superior, Father Brian, often said, smiling at his young protégé, whom he loved with a father's heart. Father Brian knew Joe's love for kids was his greatest gift, that it was healing balm to the youth in their congregation and in their community. Deep down, he saw Father Joe as *his* mentor in relating to kids, simply gifted at it.

It didn't matter in God's sight who was the teacher and who was the student, Father Brian believed. Besides, kids didn't care how much you knew until they knew how much you cared. And the kids at Good Shepherd Parish knew Father Joe cared. *You should have made a lot more priests from this mold, Father*, the senior priest prayed.

Father Joe took the youth group camping, hiking, fishing, and swimming in the Hudson River. "Meet 'em where they live, if you want to see God living in them," he counseled baffled parents. Everyone, including the children, knew Father Joe had a kid alive in him, a very engaging one indeed. His coal black mane always looked like he saw no sense in the bother of owning a comb. Smiling soft brown eyes belied the kindness of his soul.

~   ~   ~

Peter caught up with Father Joe riding his bike near the school playground one sultry August afternoon, basketball jammed in his basket. "Father Joe, what's happenin'?" Peter called out. Something about this man always made Peter smile a little. Hope, maybe? An adult who was fun, who listened, who was not preachy? Who simply liked him as he was?

"Hey, 'ject!" Father Joe shouted irreverently. *This kid is an angry little mirror-me*, he reminded himself. *I gotta watch this one carefully*. His booming voice always sounded too loud for close quarters, whatever the quarters.

"Who are you hidin' from now, trouble?" Father Joe ruffled the boy's coiffed hair.

Peter ducked, grinning. "You bum. Git offa my doo." He brushed back his hair with his fingers, feigning irritation.

Father Joe smiled on his young buddy with deep affection. "'T'sup, slick? Don't be wastin' my valuable time."

Peter cut to the point. "Father Joe, I, uh, got a priestly question. My sister Anika, the little one—she goes out to this big rock all the time, says she's communing with God. Is that too weird or is it a girl thing? I figured you might know. But please don't tell anybody I asked."

"I hear you on the privacy bit, kid. Never any sweat on that. That's our job, us priests." He parked his bike and sat on the curb, massaging his knees. Peter sat down beside him, chewing on a hangnail.

"You say she sits on a rock and communes with God? Wow, Pete. You know, she might just be a pint-sized mystic. That means somebody who has real encounters with God. Not so unusual in the history of the church, where many of the known mystics hang out, but otherwise they're pretty scarce in the world. More likely, we just don't know much about this because it's not talked about a lot. I'll bet they've been around on every street corner the whole world over. Some old, some young, all kinds of people. But some of them got tortured and burned at the stake for this in the Dark Ages so it's pretty hush-hush. Scares people, even people in the church."

"No kiddin', Father Joe? I figured you'd know. I can't tell anybody else, but I kinda want to protect her, you know? But I was scared for her . . . it seems kind of crazy." Peter shifted on the hard concrete.

"Yes, that's your job, Pete—to protect younger ones, especially girls, especially sisters. I like that spirit in you. Kinda tough, kinda soft. First-class brother." Father Joe sensed an undercurrent in Peter, so he waited quietly.

"Aw, I dunno. But she's kind of alone in our family, being the youngest. Nobody pays much attention to her." Peter rubbed his temple, scared to be telling such forbidden family business but needing to unload. He glanced sideways at Father Joe, who appeared to be listening carefully. "Thanks,

Father Joe. It helps. Promise you won't even tell Father Brian? I'd be a dead duck if my mom found out I was talking to anyone about family stuff."

Father Joe nodded. "Yeah, that would be the end of you as we know you, buddy." He chuckled, "Just kidding. You have my word. Now how about a couple of hoops?"

"If you can take the punishment . . ." Peter jumped up and grabbed his ball, hollering over his shoulder, dribbling in to sink a layup shot. Father Joe huffed up behind him, grabbed the ball and spun, sinking an easy one-hander over his shoulder.

Peter's eyes flew open wide at the skill. "Hey, you're really hot today."

Father Joe loved this part of his job, when he could interact with the young ones, hear their stories, play on their turf, and be a kid among kids. He knew if he wanted to be effective, he had to hang around where the kids were to find out what was on their minds. He sensed there was a whole lot more beneath the surface of Peter's story.

When two of Peter's basketball buddies arrived, they played two-on-two until Father Joe had to get to a meeting.

"Thanks for keeping this old man juiced up, guys."

"Bye, Father Joe. Thanks for . . . you know . . . everything." Peter took a breather.

When Father Joe left, the friends stopped in midcourt. "Did you say *Father* Joe, Pete? He's a priest? But he doesn't wear a collar, just jeans and that old BU t-shirt."

"Yeah, and a real guy, like fun and easy to talk to."

"Can we play with him again sometime, Pete?"

"I'll see what I can do, guys." *I like the way this is going*, Peter thought. *Pretty cool for a priest. Maybe, just maybe, somebody up there likes me after all.*

17

Peter

Father Joe watched Peter, muscular at thirteen, practice his specialty layup shot and thought about the boy's potential. Peter had the goods as a scorer. He was gaining height and muscle bulk and had the killer instinct of an athlete. But his silent rage was troubling, a look that said, "Bring it on."

By now, Peter's grades had slipped to Bs and Cs. He showed no interest in anything but basketball. He played hooky some days, had little respect for authority except Father Joe and his mother, and rarely bothered turning in homework. He stayed in trouble with Carlos, who wasn't around much.

Sally found research in a parenting book that claimed the father's influence was the strongest force for adolescent boys. She despaired at that dismal prognosis for her silent, angry son. There was no reasoning with Carlos, whose drinking continued to progress. He had a yellowish look now that Sally knew meant liver damage. He brushed it off. "Mexicans are dark-skinned, have you noticed, Americana?"

Sally called Father Joe after Peter's first ninth-grade report card arrived, fearing this report could detonate the bomb between Carlos and Peter. "Father Joe, I hate to impose, but you're my best ally in this war zone. Whatever can I do to protect Peter from his dad's explosion?"

"Sally, I love that boy, you know I do. I try to keep God's greater love for him uppermost in my heart. God's working things out in His own time, which He will reveal when it's right. What's that saying . . . 'God's never late, but He's often not early'? The waiting is a bear sometimes. Pray for both of them and watch."

"Father Joe, I don't even want to think what I'd do without you! I feel so scared for Peter, and it makes me hate Carlos and feel guilty for staying with him. I know that's all wrong in God's sight, but man! Such a battle in my own heart. Thanks so much."

"Sally. It's human to hate what Carlos is doing when your wise ways work so much better. This is about Carlos's denial, not who he is. He gives away his best to the booze because he thinks it's more powerful than he is, a kind of refuge. I watched booze kill my father, and his father, and several of my uncles and brothers seem hopelessly addicted in spite of all that. It's taking Carlos's life, gradually. And the crazy part is, underneath all the unnecessary pain he's creating, he's a good soul."

Father Joe waited as Sally snuffled on the line, respecting her tears as necessary release for healing.

"I've gone to God in prayer more often about this stinkin' disease than anything else on the planet, Sally-my-dear. My prayers sound something like 'What the hell did You mean by putting spirits on the earth? Lousy pun if You don't mind my saying so—spirits that take away the Holy Spirit from a man, even a whole family if they're not as smart as my Miss Sally. What kind of plan is that? Explain that to me, Father God.'"

"What'd you get?" she murmured.

Father Joe chuckled. "Wise guy said, 'Did the addicts have to drink the whole lake at one sitting?' I hate that He has a sense of humor some days."

Sally burst out laughing. "You're a hoot and a half, Father Joe. You never miss!"

~　~　~~

Sally greeted Peter coming in from school, handing him a little sack of cookies.

"Father Joe asked if you could drop by, love." She reached out to touch his face, but he ducked, rarely letting her touch him anymore. His shoulders were bunched up in anger. *If he juts that bottom lip out anymore, a bird's gonna shit on it.* Her own grannie's words made her chuckle when he was gone.

He grabbed his ball and the cookies and went out to the shed for his bike, riding off with a terse "See ya."

"You wanted to see me, Father Joe?" Peter asked testily as he flopped down on Father Joe's floor, putting the cookies by the priest.

"Just want to see how you're doin', pal. You've been a bit of a stranger lately," Father Joe began warmly. "'Course, I've been busy too. I miss ya, is all. How's it going?"

"Same old crap, different day, Father Joe. I got a bit of a headache starting up. Don't feel much like talking. How about I listen to you for a change?" He rubbed his temples, ritching around on his backside, eyes closed.

Father Joe saw his opening. He had heard a nasty rumor about the neighbor, Jack Storrs, and knew Peter had spent some time with him. Closing his eyes, he sought wisdom in prayer. *Please, God, be in my words and thoughts and guide this conversation with Your grace. Help. Thanks.* Peter saw Father Joe's lips move, his eyes closed.

"Sorry about your head, Pete." He looked kindly at the boy. He munched on a cookie, offering the sack to Peter. "Here, help yourself," handing the sack over to Peter, who took it, reached in for a cookie, mumbling a thanks.

"Maybe you can help me out here a little then. I got somethin' on my mind. And thank your mom for her great cookies—that woman can *cook* now."

"Shoot, Father Joe." Peter kept rubbing his temples, head down, urging Father Joe to get to the point, get this over with so he could go home to the solitude of his room. "I'm listening."

"Okay, buddy. So, my young cousin, Allie, from Somerset? Turns out she's your sister Anika's best friend. THAT Allie. Small world, huh! I hadn't seen her since she was little. I didn't know she was living here in Albany— my Uncle Vinny told me last weekend. Her folks got killed in a car wreck when she was two. Turns out they were drinking as usual. So my sister's brother-in-law Tom and his wife have been raising her."

"Yeah, Anika and I knew Allie's story except the part about her being your cousin. She's a great kid. Anika's Siamese twin. They're always together." Peter smiled a little. "Your cousin, huh?" Peter waited to see where Father Joe was headed with this.

"Yeah, that's it. So—I heard last weekend that another cousin got a little too friendly with her during a family visit, and the boy's father walked in on it. Daggone, that girl had a lot dumped on her by my crazy family." He paused, shaking his head, taking a bite of his cookie. "Hope his father didn't tear him apart." He munched a cookie absently.

"It gripped my heart some, which is why I had to get it off my chest, so thanks, bud. Maybe it's because of the shame I felt for fooling around with *my* cousin." He shook his head as if to shake off the memory. "I didn't talk about it for many a year because I thought I was a despicable monster for letting it happen. Now I know it happens in many kids' lives, especially in alcoholic families. And none of us has to feel alone with it. It's usually just curiosity and normal kids exploring everything." He paused, chewing on his cookie. *Careful now, Joe.* Peter nodded.

"Unless it's mean or it's an older person doing it to a younger one. Then it's despicable, criminal. Convicted perpetrators go to jail for a long time. But nobody talks about it like I couldn't so it festers in the dark, doing a whole lot of damage to our hearts." Father Joe let this rest in silence, giving Peter a way through if he wanted.

Peter stopped rubbing his temples, hands still beside his face. *Oh my god—he knows. Oh shit! That's what he's been leading up to. I can't let this show or I'm as good as dead. Oh MA-an, I'm in such deep shit. Why didn't I see this coming?*

Father Joe dug a thumb into an aching leg muscle. He knew his young friend felt all alone with this, just like with the pain of his father's drunken raging. *Poor kid. Father,* **please** *help Pete get this darkness out of his heart and into the open.*

"Pete, I love you, buddy. You know I'd do anything for you." Father Joe got up and sat on the floor beside Peter and ran his fingers through his mane, looking at Peter closely. He waited for the boy to gather his courage, hoping he wouldn't bolt. Peter saw the compassion out of the corner of his eye.

"Father Joe, I—uh—gotta . . ." Peter burst out crying and fell into Father Joe's arms, sobbing hard, releasing a load of hideous shame. Father Joe tenderly wiped Peter's nose and eyes with his handkerchief, silently giving thanks for the gift of healing tears. He kissed the boy's head again and again, his strong arms enfolding the boy.

"I—oh, God—sometimes—uh—a guy I know—and sometimes—oh, mann—I touch Anika—oh, GO-ODD!" Peter choked out his shame with heart-ripping sobs.

Father Joe held him tight, rocking him gently back and forth.

"It's okay, buddy," Father Joe said very softly. "God forgives you, now that you've had the guts to let it out, and so do I. So who are you not to forgive yourself? Let it all out, pal. This is what tears are for . . . so we can clean our hearts out. I cry like a baby sometimes and don't even know why. God's own plumbing system, release valve for healing us. You can tell me about it if you want, or not. But now the big thing is you don't need to do it some more. All those tears say you've been carrying around a ton of shame, huh? It's not your fault, Pete. It's the adult creep's fault, not yours. Not at *all*."

He stroked Peter's head as the boy buried himself in his chest, ashamed of letting Father Joe see his face. When his tears began to subside, he remembered another incident and deeper layers washed out. He feared his pain was bottomless.

They sat together for a long time. After a while, Peter felt something lighten in him. "Father Joe," he murmured into the priest's chest. He felt the priest's arms loosen a little and heard his whispered "Yeah, bud."

"I feel so bad I can't stand it. I feel like a filthy monster who doesn't deserve to breathe."

"I know, son, I know. Cuz I did too." He rocked Peter like a baby, feeling deeply grateful for this sacred moment of trust. He closed his eyes and prayed deep thanks in his heart.

"We don't ever have to speak of this again unless you want to, little buddy. But if you do it some more, your shame will get worse. God will weep more if you go hurting yourself with the same mistake. He hates your suffering, and Anika's, and even that guy's. Give Him a chance and see if His love doesn't take this burden away."

"What else *can* I do, Father? I'm done. That's it. It's too hideous to face you with this." Peter shook his head in wonder that this terrible burden could possibly be lifted. He knew one thing for sure—his furtive sex activity was over.

Father Joe knew he had to report this to Father Brian and discuss the legal requirements. He knew he was in over his head and prayed for guidance. But for now, Peter . . . He shifted to lighter ground. "And next time you wanna bust my butt on the basketball court . . ." Joe ruffled Peter's hair, then dug a knuckle into his scalp. Peter winced out of his grasp and grinned.

"You *are* getting a little feeble on the court, old man." Peter sniffed, wiping his nose on Father Joe's wet hanky.

"Yeah? Let's go, tough talker." Father Joe grabbed his basketball and ran out the door with Peter in close pursuit. "This is where men settle things, buddy pal. Old, huh?" he huffed.

After Peter's confession, Father Joe paid a surprise visit to Jack Storrs one evening. Jack let him in, apprehensively. The priest's visit could only mean one thing; but Jack was caught by surprise and by propriety from his Catholic upbringing. After a few get-acquainted exchanges, Father Joe got to the point. "Jack, there's a rumor going around that could be damaging to your reputation, so I thought you had the right to know. The Father has given us the gift of sensuality alongside the discretion to respect others, especially young impressionable ones. Our Father is not about judging but about healing us. All of us." Father Joe leaned his elbows on his thighs, pausing to give Jack space to speak.

Jack cleared his throat, rubbing his palms together. "Well, sir. Very graciously put, Father. You could have delivered this message very differently, and I appreciate that. I give you my word I will heed your warning, with all due respect." Jack Storrs moved to Troy, closer to work, and began attending another parish. He sought treatment for pedophilia. He acknowledged in counseling that he'd dodged a powerful bullet because of the grace of one wise young Irish priest.

18

Cassandra—1953

Cassandra, now twenty, came down to the kitchen on a drizzly November Saturday morn. She poured herself a cup of coffee, looked at her mother's faded dress, washed gray, and her tired face, and flashed on an idea.

"C'mon, Mama, get your coat. You look fine as you are. Do not say no to me. We're goin'."

"But Cass . . . the stew . . ."

"Turn it off. C'mon, Mom, I'm not kidding. First breakfast. Then shopping." Cass took her Mom's waist and hand and danced her around the floor in a little waltz singing "Downtown." Sally hooted with her.

Sally smoothed her skirt. "Cass, honey, I have no money."

"I know, Mom. But I do. And I want to spend it on you. Don't waste your breath arguing. I got paid by that tightwad of a boss I slave for—all the money he makes at that store and doesn't he make every penny squeak—so we're goin' downtown. You deserve a break and a bright new dress. Maybe even shoes to match. What would you think of that?"

They got in Cass's car, the redhead's jaw set in familiar determination that her mama knew well. She hit the gas pedal and burned a little rubber, smiling at her own dramatics. Cass's red hair burned bright. Her eyes flashed. She had fire to give to her mama who had little of her own left.

"I can't do much to help you deal with that deadbeat of a husband, Mom, but we can spend some of my paycheck that's burning a hole in my pocket on you. We're goin' DOWNtown." She grinned a bodacious grin at her mom.

"Don't you want to save your money to get your own place, honey?" Sally said, putting others first as usual.

"Oh, Mom, think of yourself for once, can't you? You do such a good job taking care of our family and he's SO hard on you. Is he *really* worth selling your soul for? Martyr-mama? Dag*gone*. You're *way* too pretty and cool for that brand of deadness, Mom."

Sally glanced at Cass for permission to turn the rear view mirror on herself, wondering how she looked to Cass and the world. She recognized with an immediate jolt what had inspired Cass to this sudden shopping impulse. Looking back at her were dull eyes, pale skin, the face of depression with a capital D. Her mother. However had that crept in—the very face she swore she'd *never* wear.

She saw *tired* opposite Cass's bright face and youthful vigor. Lifeless. What had she become? She wasn't fooling anyone, not even herself. There it was right out in the open for God and all the people to see. Her old bright spirit gone the way of the booze.

This just might be my moment to break this cycle of madness, Sally admitted, staring into the mirror. *I'm way too scared on my own, don't even have a clue how, but if Cass will prod me . . . I get that my very life depends on what I decide here.*

"Cass, baby, is it *really* possible for me? I mean, to get my spark back? Grow a backbone? Do you *really* think so?" Excitement pulsed through her; then terror. Then fresh hope. Back and forth they wrestled as she stared in her eyes.

"I KNOW, Mom. Not think. It's time for you to wake up and fly out of the turkey pen to soar with the eagles. Only then will you break this pattern, because you're the one choosing it. Sorry, sweets, but you are. Just like I chose Bobby the snake to wake me up to my insanity . . . letting *any*body abuse me—nutso." She tapped her forehead. She eased the car into the right lane and slowed down, giving Sally time for her own sorting.

After a bit she ventured, "Mom. Darlin'. I've been going to Al-Anon with Angie during lunch hour for over a month now." Cass adjusted her rearview mirror, then brushed back a curl from her forehead. "She told me what's been eating at her finally. Her dad's a drunk too. We got to talking one day, and it was amazing how we feel so much the same about so many things. She took me to my first meeting because she could hear my pain, and her therapist made her go. Mom, those people understand what our lives have been like, the insanity of living with an active drunk because they've been there."

"What's Al-Anon, honey? Father Joe said something about it the other day."

Cassandra checked her mom's face for permission to pursue this further. She knew how scary it was for her mom to name this nightmare. Once spoken, it was real, out in the open. Cass had been terrified to go to her first meeting, and she knew her stakes were peanuts compared to her mom's. This was the motherlode of fear: Wake the sleeping elephant in the living room at your own peril. You can't know where it will spin out. You know only one thing—it's out of the control of silence—the *illusion* of control, that is.

Sally pondered this slowly. Cassandra watched her pained expression. "Who's Al-Anon for? And what do you talk about at your meetings? The drunks? The pain?" A smile twitched at her lips. "Killing them in their sleep?"

Cassandra laughed heartily, relieved that Sally could laugh at it all, knowing from her own tears and laughter that both marked the beginning of healing.

"Actually, we hardly ever talk about them, Mom, except as we admit our own crazy responses to the craziness. We talk about our own progress and slips. We tell on ourselves and get perspective on our own lives, not the alcoholics we all came in wanting to kill, or fix. If we whine, pretty quick they let us know gently that we're here for ourselves, that the alcoholic has his or her own choices that are none of our business. Seemed crazy at first, but then I began to see people smiling and laughing after describing really tough situations, and talking about their Higher Power—you know, God. And I started to look at me, why I pick alcoholics to date. Let's not even *talk* about Bobby the snake. I'm lucky I didn't land in the hospital."

Cass looked in the mirror to check before changing lanes. She turned left at the light, pulling into a parking spot in front of their coffee shop. "Perfecto!" She laughed. "Thanks for the ideal parking place, angels. You're good." She winked at her mom. "I knew if I asked . . ."

Cass sat still, reflective. "One young woman, about thirty-five, came to her first meeting last week. She cried through the whole meeting. We just gave her the Kleenex box and encouraged her to get it out, said we'd all done that at first. At the end, she spoke, whispered actually, that her son was grappling with the disease like her ex had, his father, now sober ten years. She didn't know how to fix her son, she cried. Poor soul was in a ton of pain and guilt. 'What did I do so wrong to cause this?'"

"One of the old wise women in our group said so kindly, 'You didn't cause this, and you don't fix him, honey, bless your heart. You learn to deal with you—your fear, your guilt. We'll help you if you let us, but you have to take the initiative for your recovery. Man, good stuff, hunh?" She touched her mom's leg lightly, turned off the engine, and looked inquiringly at Sally, eyebrows high.

"Let's do it," Sally nodded, checking her reflection one last time. *A baby step brighter . . .*

Cass cozied into a booth, grabbing her mom's two hands and squeezing them as they sat face-to-face. She ordered coffees and blueberry muffins, winking at their similar tastes and the shared goodness of this stolen time alone. Sally felt her heart soften in this warm sharing time.

Cassandra gently scratched the corner of her itchy right eye with her pinky nail. "Thanks for your usual patient listening through that mess with Bobby while we were dating, Mom. I know it wasn't much fun for you, hearing that story, especially when you're living it too. But you were smart. You trusted me figure it out myself."

"I blame myself for your struggles, honey, because I chose to stay in an unhealthy marriage. I know it has scarred you kids. I'm *so* sorry." Sally put her palms together and rubbed them back and forth to gather her thoughts. She lowered her voice, looking directly in Cass's eyes. "It just seemed best to keep the family together," Sally said in a tight voice. "My mom tried as long as she could, but Dad left anyway. I give her a lot of credit now for how hard she worked—two jobs, never any time for herself, never a break. Back then, I didn't understand all she was up against and just thought she didn't care about us. I was such a brat." She wrinkled her nose and chuckled, chin in her hands.

Sally recalled her mother's silence in the face of alcoholic insanity—she thought her mother a spineless jellyfish, scared of a stupid stumbling drunk. Why didn't she just leave the madman? Then he left, and she watched her mom struggle through great hardship for years. So she figured it was better for her own kids to have a home and the stability of at least one loving parent taking care of business.

"Now I understand much of what my mother lived, keeping it all together for us kids. I guess I've slowly turned into the martyr she was." She felt a rush of pure white-hot anger alongside a flash of new insight. "Dear *God*. The *very* thing I tried to avoid . . ."

Cass saw the reddening flush on her mother's face. "What's happening, Mom? What's coming up?" She stirred her coffee patiently, loving this intimacy.

"It's just that I see these same themes running through our alcoholic families—not just ours but other women I talk with at church. Where does it ever end? Are we all doomed to repeat a lifetime of our birth family's drama? Dumb plan—I can't believe a loving God would allow this for so many of us. And I *hate* that I have brought this on you kids, repeating the very scene I set out to conquer."

"Mom, we all just do what we know. It's human nature. That's how this stinking disease works. They call it the family disease in Al-Anon because it affects us as much as the alcoholic, only differently. It's why I keep going toward alcoholics and addicts, though it's totally unconscious at the time. I heard somebody at a meeting say, 'Do I wear a sign across my forehead, alcoholics and addicts welcome here?' I didn't even see Bobby drink for months after we met. Slimeball. He lured me in and then blasted me. Never saw it coming. Man, do I feel stupid."

Cass looked down at her empty cup. The waitress came by to refill their cups. "You ladies like some real breakfast?" she asked, friendly, picking up their muffin plates. "Out for a mom-and-daughter getaway?"

Cass shook her head to breakfast, smiling at the waitress. "No thanks. I'm full. And yeah, we're off to a shopping spree. Just for the fun of it. Look out, *world*."

Sally nodded when the waitress left. "I remember the deal with Bobby all too well, hon. I smelled booze on him the first time we met, but you said, 'No, he doesn't drink.' Come to think of it, I made those excuses for Carlos to my mom too."

"Yeah, Mom, see what I mean? You and the whole town knew Bobby drank before I did. No wonder I have such a hard time with relationships. Look at my track record. Bobby, Jack, Freddy—"

"Yes, but it's getting better. Freddy held a job for more than a month, right?" Sally laughed and took Cass's hand, grateful that they could be so honest and open with each other, even laugh together at their mistakes, their "research."

"Jack wouldn't talk about any of his family. Even *I* knew that spelled trouble. Then he started blaming me for everything, including the poverty in India and his work troubles. Said I spent money frivolously. The blame game." She nodded her thanks to the waitress for fresh coffees. "Turns out he was the child of two alcoholics."

Sally laughed. "Yeah, I remember. He was jealous of any attention you got from anyone. Maybe he thought that if you weren't so pretty, he wouldn't have to be so threatened. He looked like a time bomb every night he waited for you to come downstairs." They laughed at the memories.

Sally got quiet. Cassandra watched.

"Your dad's good at that too, as you well know. Always something terrible about to happen and always somebody else's fault. You know what I think is at the bottom of it? I think he feels so guilty about his drinking and even about himself as a person that he has to cover by blaming somebody else. Low self-esteem, is that what that's called?" She pursed her lips and looked down at her hands, feeling the sadness now.

"Good point, Mom. That's something we on the other side of the aisle share with the alcoholic. Our disease—self-esteem in the toilet." Cassandra let out a sarcastic snort, then frowned. "Living our lives in the shadow of others, most especially the alcoholic's. Like we're living secondhand, not even aware of our own needs."

Sally cocked her head, looking surprised. "I never knew you felt insecure about yourself, hon. You've always acted so confident—captain of the varsity cheerleaders, vice president of your class, active in school clubs, lots of friends . . ."

"That's my cover, Mom. Acting. I've always thought I had to prove myself, never be caught off guard or out of control. Stay busy. They say it's classic child of an alcoholic thinking. I played the hero role, always trying to look good, always trying to please you and Dad, be the role model for the younger kids. Most of the time, I felt like a chicken with my head cut off. Still do, truth be told. I don't really know who I am yet, or who I want to be when I grow up."

"Honey, don't you think that's true for a lot of people, struggling to know ourselves? I feel the same way, even at my ripe old age of thirty-eight. And I've heard Marymoll say it's a lifelong journey. Adults wrestle with those questions all the time. But we don't always admit it."

"Yeah, Mom, it is normal, and human. But us Al-Anons ramp it up about eight notches and dance it around our ears." Cass laughed loud, pushing back in her seat. Her mother burst out laughing with her. They were both surprised at the open easy tone this tricky conversation was taking.

Cass pushed a little further. "If you'd ever like to come to a meeting with us, I know Angie would be thrilled too. She tries to get her mom to come but that woman's got a mind like a brick wall. I'm so glad you and I can talk so well. You're my hero, Mom. Thanks. I don't know how you've done so well, but . . ." She reached for her mom's hands. " . . . forever thanks for being our rock, Mom. I hope someday I'm half the woman you are."

"You guys are my rocks too, babe. Thanks for opening up this can of worms. Maybe I will come with you girls. It seems to be doing you a lot of good—you're easier, happier, more relaxed lately. Maybe Al-Anon is why." She paused a moment, rearranged her watch, considering.

"Okay, I'll try it. I'd be a fool not to when you're already showing such nice results."

"Great, Mom! This Wednesday, then. Six o'clock at the Methodist church on Allen St."

"You've got a date, girl." She smoothed her flyaway hair, hoping Cass hadn't forgotten her offer of a shopping trip. She loved this new way of sharing with her daughter.

"Ready to roll out shopping, old girl?" Cass hadn't forgotten.

"You're on!"

19

Sally—1953

The next month, Cass was at her Al-Anon meeting talking with Angie, now her roommate, when Sally surprised them by walking in, looking around tentatively. Cass jumped up to hug her, nudging Angie with a little elbow look-who's-here jab.

Cass walked her mom to a comfortable couch, then stood holding her around the waist. "You came! I'm so proud of you!" She squeezed her mom's side.

Angie slid in on Sally's other side to hug her, saying, "You are so courageous! Wish my mom would come. You made my night, Miss Sally." She swiped at her eyes, laughing away her tears.

Sally smiled at their welcome. "So how's the new apartment, gals? Settled in?"

The chairperson called out to start the meeting with "Let's have a moment of silence followed by the Serenity Prayer." The three women plopped down together.

After the usual reading of the welcome, first-name introductions, the reading of the twelve steps and the tradition of the month, someone shared a reading about the first step—"Admitted we were powerless over alcohol, that our lives had become unmanageable"—highlighting humility as a significant first-step characteristic. Enlightening discussion followed, punctuated with the balm of laughter.

The word "powerless" floated around in Sally's head like a whole new concept. There was a lot of honest sharing Sally could relate to. She was astonished by the common experiences—how she'd lived with the same feelings these folks were describing so openly, so courageously. She felt connected, as though these people had been reading from her journal. At the end of the hour when the chairperson asked, "Are there any burning desires to share before we close?"

Sally felt an internal nudge. She squirmed in her seat, then spoke barely above a whisper.

"My name is Sally. Thanks for your warm welcome. I'm amazed by what I'm hearing—so many of the same things I've felt—and by the honesty I've heard here tonight. And the reading helped me see my own choice to stay as humility rather than cowardice. I've always feared I was too scared to leave my alcoholic. But actually, I chose to stay for the kids' sake. I see now from what's been said here that I was choosing stability for them, and that's what kept me sane. I grew up without a dad, and I didn't want that for my kids. Thank you for the whole new understanding of this. What a relief." She smiled a shy, radiant smile.

Cass's heart about burst with gladness for her mother's courage. She beamed at Sally, eyes leaking. Several people noticed and asked afterward if that was her mother. She nodded, choked up. "It doesn't get any better than this," she told them. "And it doesn't have to."

After the meeting, Cass suggested the three go out for coffee and pie with several friends to talk more personally. Sally heard more authentic sharing, more ownership of one's own choices, which she found rare in the world. No gossip, no whining, just honesty and openness and plenty of laughter. She wanted to come back, though it felt scary. She thought of Peter and his silent fury and thought this work might help her deal with him.

She said to Cass, "I see why you're growing wise here, why you love this program, hon. Let's see where this goes. Don't be surprised if I—"

"I'd be overjoyed, Mom. Another good thing for us to share. Thanks so much for coming. Come back if you want, anytime. I'll gladly pick you up."

Sally drove slowly home, thinking of her new understanding of humility and powerlessness. Somewhere in those concepts she sensed new freedom.

She dropped over to Marymoll's for coffee. "Can I run something by you, sweet?"

"Any ol' time, me luv. What's on yer mind?" Marymoll was always open and ready to listen, no matter her own troubles of the day.

"You have such a great pair of ears! So here's what I heard in Al-Anon last night: that we are powerless over alcoholism. Exactly what I did *not* want to hear. I thought they might tell me how to get Carlos to quit drinking. They said that wasn't our business. And *then* they did a reading about humility—something like 'Now I climb down off my ladder of judgment and join a worldwide circle of love and support.' Marymoll, does that make sense to you?"

"Well, m' dearie, it makes all the sense in th' world t' me. But only after I tried ever' dirty trick in th' book t' beat th' drink outa my Seamus." She laughed 'til the tears came, slapping her thigh. Sally got to laughing hysterically with her.

As Marymoll's funny bone settled itself, she grew pensive. "Yeah, that humility stuff came hard t' me, me luv. Felt like the biggest mountain Gawd ever asked me t' climb, downright impossible. An' wasn't Seamus th' one with th' drinkin' problem, an' meself all innocent and perfeck? 'Land sakes, Gawd, I said t' Him. This ain't fair."

"So how'd you learn your inspiring humility then?" Sally asked, picking up crumbs with her finger.

"I didn't, dear. Gawd did. He said t' me, 'Marymoll, luv, mind yer business'. Jes' like that. So I picked meself up off the floor an' told 'im, 'Well, sir, I guess I'll do jes' that,' an' I stomped on outa there. An' He give me some humility pie right there like He does—straightaway I got splashed wi' mud by a car goin' by." She stood up painfully to refill their coffees. "I was sech a hardhead then. Saucy one. Not kind like ye are."

Sally nodded her thanks. "I can't imagine you being unkind but I'll believe it if you tell me it's so, dear one. Maybe if I ask, He'll teach me, d'you think?" She checked her watch. "Better run. Kids'll be home in a minute. Love you, dear. Bye for now." She hugged her mentor and walked home with fresh thoughts to chew on.

20

Peter

School had always been a mixed bag for Peter. Bright and curious, new information came easily to him; but emotionally he felt disconnected, like boring school was something he had to do well or face dire consequences at home. So he showed up and went through the motions, waiting for something real to present itself. He was intriguing to his schoolmates, perhaps because he always held something back. His dark good looks and quick humor didn't hurt his image with his peers or girls. Teachers tried to get him to open up, but he was not buying. He remained aloof. Trust was a rare commodity to be earned over time for Peter.

The only adult he opened up to besides Sally, rarely now, was Father Joe, who walked a careful, respectful razor's edge, knowing how easily Peter could be spooked, the fragile bond shattered. The real fun in Peter's life was on the basketball court, so Father Joe met him there, playing fast and hard. Peter loved it at full throttle. No mercy, just real and tough. He grew in skill and passion for the game, absorbing stats and players, talking it with his friends, watching it on television when they got one in 1952.

Father Joe asked for God's guidance with Peter often through the days, knowing Peter's struggles were so like his own adolescent trials that he had to be careful not to project. He knew he could only support the boy but not fix the situation. It kept him challenged, mindful of his own odyssey through dark growing-up years. So it was sweet relief to let it all out on the basketball court, pounding and twisting and shooting and leaping. There it was all real—just guts and the occasional taste of glory.

To avoid punishment at home, Peter was always alert to his father's moods and whereabouts. His mother rode the fence to protect him without overplaying her hand and setting Carlos off. Her steadiness was grounding for Peter, more than she or he realized. But sometimes when Carlos would be particularly brutal and she would keep silent, not fighting back, he would feel confused. As he grew older, he felt the wisdom of her holding the peace, keeping things from getting worse. Carlos was flat out impossible. He would eventually give up for lack of a worthy adversary and go sleep it off.

Peter kept his own counsel and waited.

One hot September morning of his senior year of high school, he and Father Joe were on the court early before the heat cranked up. Pete sank a hook shot and stopped for a breather. He tossed the ball back and forth, deciding how to say what he was thinking. Father Joe waited.

"Any way you see I could go to college, Big Guy? Maybe work cycle mechanics to pay my way? I've been thinkin' I'll go to state, maybe major in English lit. Don't yet know what to do with my life. Maybe I can figure it out there. Whaddya think?" Peter dribbled the ball low to the ground, left handed, then right, waiting.

"Good plan, bud," Father Joe huffed, letting Peter pace the conversation. "That's what college is for, to help you figure out how to work at something you love." Father Joe had always steered him toward college, knowing how bright he was, and that once he started he'd likely get hooked and find his way.

"I like to read the big writers like Kierkegaard, Tolstoy, and Plato. I loved Plato's cave. The way he went into the cave and saw all the images of human behavior for what they were and came out knowing the meaning of life? Fired me up. I think about Kerouac, how powerful a writer he was, and Hemingway. And Dostoyevsky. Jack London. Those guys hook me. Otherwise, school is a crushing bore."

"You read these big shots in school or on your own?" Father Joe was impressed by Peter's breadth of reading. He showed a sharp seeking intelligence.

They sat on the side of the court, fanning themselves with pieces of cardboard the wind had blown in. Peter dribbled the ball between his legs, searching for the right words.

"Some of both. Plato and London I found on my own, the others in English class." Then more quietly still, he said, "Uhm, Father Joe?"

"Yeah, bud." Father Joe turned to look straight at him. *Pay-attention time.*

"Think I could teach English?" he whispered huskily as if the words were in danger of getting caught in his throat.

"Pete, I think you could do that well, *really* well. That's a great plan. When you do what you love, the way opens and you sail through obstacles because you *want* that. I could see you being a role model for inquiring minds, a sharp teacher. It's amazing you've hung in there with boring school and tough home life—a miracle, for real. You didn't give up, didn't turn to the street for your kicks. So you more than most will relate to kids, Pete. They'll know you speak their language. Maybe you're beginning to sniff out your special calling." Father Joe rubbed his calves, liking this thinking.

Peter stared at him, daring to believe. Until now he'd survived, gotten by. He rotated the basketball slowly, contemplating new possibilities. "You mean I could teach kids to believe in themselves like you do for me?"

"Pete, you will break ground in kids' minds and in your own." Father Joe stared into the future, visualizing Peter as popular guide to many young minds. "Man, bud, this feels like gold. You've got it!" He curbed his tongue to let this be Peter's dream and not take over.

What seemed like hours later, Peter choked out, "Thanks, old coot. If it hadn't been for you and Mom, I'd have been in the boys' home long ago."

"Yeah, well, I needed a basketball buddy." Father Joe grinned. "Keep me hustlin'."

Peter began his application to Albany State the next day, choosing English lit for his major. He wrote a preadmission essay that he hesitantly showed Father Joe. "How's this sound, if you don't mind, Big Guy?"

Father Joe read it carefully. It was rough but showed the boy's potential. "Flesh it out just a little bit more, bud. Play with it, fill in some of the gaps. Write the sentence between the sentences. You show a real gift here, Pete, a flair for writing."

"You're never satisfied." Peter grinned.

"Yeah, well, you sound like you're trying to drink from a fire hose." Joe tweaked the boy's nose. "Give 'em a pound of flesh. Your writing is really good, and that's what will get you in. So embellish it a little. Strut your stuff."

Peter was accepted at Albany State College. Finally challenged and engaged, he loved the literature if not the requisite freshman courses nor the living at home. He puzzled to Father Joe one day on the court, "Why do you think I let Dad get to me so bad, Father Joe? I see that he's just a miserable drunk, yet he sets my teeth on edge quicker than anyone in the world. Does that ever go away?"

"It will, son, in time. Maybe pay less attention to him? Let's take it out on the court. Pound it out of you."

Peter grabbed his ball and whipped around in a spin that nearly toppled Father Joe.

"Oh, sorry, old man."

"I'll show you sorry!" Father Joe grabbed the ball and dribbled it close to the ground fast and hard. Peter smiled as he watched Father Joe throw his whole body and soul into the moment.

"Why couldn't this be a perfect world and you have been my dad?"

Father Joe slammed the ball at Peter's chest with a big grin. "You gonna play ball or flap your jaws? Show me how mad you are. *C'mon.*"

Peter slammed the ball around with vengeance and precision. Slowly the tension yielded as the sweat increased. He felt himself pass into a kind of euphoria.

"Ye-haaah!" Peter leaped up and sank a rim shot. "Yessss. Bastard just doesn't matter. Here. Now!"

Father Joe laughed and drove in for a dunk, which he missed. "Shit!" he hollered fiercely. "I can't make *shit* today."

Peter slacked off a notch to give Father Joe a break. "It's too hot to play here today. Buy you a soda?"

"Yeah, you can. And spare me the pity, pal."

21

College—1957

Anika turned nineteen as Peter became a man of twenty-one, both in April of 1957. Both attended Albany State College at night. Peter was a literature major with a business minor, a mechanic by day. Anika had chosen a major in psychology with a literature minor, working days as a stenographer for an insurance firm. Each was taking one or two courses per semester, inching their way through together, living at home.

"I knew you'd go for psych. You're a born shrink," Peter told her on their ride home from class one night. "You are easier to talk to than anyone our age."

Anika nodded. "Yeah, seems to be my calling. Most people seem to love to talk about themselves. But who's listening? I just seem to have the knack— and the desire." She drove slowly, enjoying being with her brother as college pals. "Still want to be a writer, then?"

"I want to, but it looks like a long hard road. Don't know if I have the talent or the endurance yet." He laughed a self-deprecating snort, flicking a cigarette out his window.

Sally had thrown a party for Peter's big twenty-first birthday and Anika's nineteenth. The kids' friends came, plus a new friend of Sally's from Al-Anon. Carlos didn't make it home that night. Marymoll sat smiling beside Father Joe, patting his knee and looking at the Mendoza children proudly. "Told ye they'd be makin' it," she teased him. "Gawd's own kids, yah?"

Peter held up his glass high in a toast. "To our manhood!" he shouted as he downed his draft beer. Cheers went up from his friends in celebration.

Father Joe raised his glass in toast. "Who'd have thunk any of you sorry rejects would live to see twenty-one!" More cheers for themselves and boo's for Father Joe.

Sally raised her wine glass. "Hear, hear! A toast to Peter's big twenty-first and Anika's nineteenth!" she said with a full heart. She wondered offhandedly where Carlos was. No one asked for him out of respect for her feelings. Nobody cared.

Cass slid up to her mom and slipped her arm around her waist. "Rudder-of-my-life," she acknowledged to a friend proudly. "Good job," Mom. Sally acknowledged the praise with new humility, deeply grateful all the kids were thriving. *Keep me humble, close to the ground, in You, please, Sir. Thank You for this night from the bottom of my heart—they're all thriving. Breathing, Marymoll would say.*

When Father Joe told Theo he was going to an important Friday night party, Theo responded with, "Go, you partyin' fool. I'll just sit here alone in the dark and suffer." He reached around behind his friend and pinched Father Joe's butt. "Shall I come over Saturday morning, then? I can stay in that motel down on the river."

"Yeah, you can do the driving for once." Father Joe grinned. Then, gratefully, he said, "I don't deserve you."

"No, it's true. You don't," Theo agreed smugly. "Nobody could."

Joe brought his face in close, pulling softly on Theo's ear, adoring him.

22

Best Friends—November 1960

Anika had worked since age eleven, doing babysitting and yard work, then at sixteen started clerking in a dress shop. Now twenty-one, she was self-reliant, partly because she was independent by nature and also because she saw she would have to provide for herself. Family resources were slim pickings, so she learned to resource her own desires.

Her best friend since fourth grade, Allie McCurrie, was studying to be a math teacher, also at Albany State College. Allie, Father Joe's cousin, was dating Jeff and living with her aunt and uncle. The girls, closer than many sisters, shared everything.

Anika had hooked up with Sly Starner at seventeen. They met through Peter who played hoops with Sly. The boys had struck up a friendship on the court, sensing their similar backgrounds. Both were natural athletes, played to win, and had killer competitive instincts. Once Sly's father had come to pick him up at the court, stumbling and slurring his words and yelling at Sly. Peter said to Sly later in private, "I know what that feels like, bud." From then on, they were allies in understanding the shadows of alcoholism.

Anika was drawn to Sly from the first time they met. She thought him ruggedly attractive and built—hard qualities for a seventeen-year-old to resist—and there was quick chemistry between them. He felt familiar to her, kind of like Peter. They'd been together except the couple of times when he took off with another girl. But he always returned to Anika. She fussed awhile, then took him back.

"Inevitable I'll take him back, damn him," she told Allie. "Can't seem to wash that jerk out of my hair. I do *try*, you know."

Allie shook her head. "No common sense. Pretty dumb for a smart girl. What is it that you see in him anyway?"

"I dunno, Al, it's just—he's just my guy, y' know? He's smart and sexy and fun and—I just love him. I do. Don't always *like* him, but . . . It's just kind of a done deal. like destiny Of course, it could just be garden-variety stupidity. Like Mom."

Allie stopped over at Anika's next day after class. "Let's go hiking Saturday, you up for it, thunder thighs?" Allie taunted. "Final exams next week. We could use some fresh mountain air before the onslaught."

"You're on, pal. I'll bring the snacks. You bring the coffee—you make great brew. Let's get up real early, see the sunrise, okay?"

Allie groaned and held her wrist backward to her forehead in a histrionic surrender. Anika rolled her eyes in reply.

It was just coming up dawn when they arrived at the parking lot by the Helderberg mountain trail. They paused to delight in the soul-nurturing spectacle of beauty. Both girls felt their hearts slide open a little in the joy of being together to watch a new day dawn. They were silenced by the view, soaking in the deep peace.

Anika spoke softly, reluctant to break in on the silence and wonder. "Al, do you think I'm crazy to love Sly? Tell the truth." She looked Allie dead in the eye.

"Oh yeah, I *do*. He's not near good enough for you. But you can't help who you love. There's something compelling about that creep for you. I've quit fighting it."

Long silence.

"Allie?"

"Yeah." A flicker of dread rang through Allie's heart. She closed her eyes.

"I think I'm pregnant." Anika was half scared and half in wonder at this bizarre turn of events.

"Oh, *shit*! I was afraid of this when you said he wouldn't protect himself. See what I mean, not good enough? Bet he did this on purpose to trap you because he knows he's beneath you. Or could it be just garden variety self-centeredness?" She groaned, shaking her head and blowing her breath out through her lips. "So. What're you gonna do?"

Anika loved that always matter-of-fact, practical quality in her friend's way of thinking—the mathematician. She saw herself as more emotional about everything, less decisive. She smiled her appreciation of Allie's direct approach.

"Thanks for not blasting me, Al. I always count on you for that, not judging me. I'm flipping my lid enough for both of us. I love Sly—that's pretty much the bottom line. Other guys just bore me. My mother would be horrified if I got an abortion. 'What would Father Brian say?'" she said in a shocked falsetto voice, mimicking the church's admonition on abortion. "I haven't told Sly yet because I wanted to think it through with you first."

"What does that tell you about your trust in Sly, babe, that you trust me more than him?" She pursed her lips and looked questioningly at Anika. "But I guess it's a little late for that. Let me have a think, Annie." Allie pondered all sides of a thing before deciding what to do. Then once she felt sure, she went with her gut, full speed ahead.

"C'mon, I think better when I'm moving." Her sandy blond ponytail contrasted with her black jacket, highlighting her smooth skin and dark brown eyes, making a beautiful picture to Anika. She felt a grateful tear leak.

"Damn, Al, you're taking this as seriously as if it were your own crisis. Thanks, love. You are *such* a good pal," she gushed, wiping at the tear. "Sometimes I don't know my own mind, Al. Scares me—ba-ad."

"Come on, goofy!" Allie played it down, mussing Anika's hair. "What would you be doin' if it were my life-changing moment?" They walked on in the quiet, listening to their footfalls on the gravel path, the wind in the trees, a crow's call.

"Okay." Allie, the strategist. "Let's look at your options. What are *you* thinking you'll do?"

Anika shot her an embarrassed look. "I knew this could happen, of course, but I got caught up in his pleasure and let it happen. Okay, more than once. Not too bright, hunh? Like my mother, always putting someone else before me. Watching you think for yourself helps me with that. It's like I don't know how. Or I don't think I deserve anything good. If I even I talk about myself, I get really ashamed, like that's just *wrong*."

"Skip the self-recrimination, please—you know I hate when you do that. You're human and you're in love. And at some level you probably wanted the pregnancy too. So lighten up. It's done, so let's do the hard facts here." Allie gazed at the sunrise, aware that she was happy being right where she was with her best friend, no matter what.

"You're right. Okay. So Sly has a decent job at Westinghouse and an apartment we could share. But he doesn't make enough to support a family. I would leave my job in a heartbeat, but not school. That's where my passion lies, in school and psychology and in my future. So how can I pull it all off, be married with a kid on just one income and stay in school?"

Allie was thinking hard, trying to get to the right questions. "Grants. Loans. It's a pretty good time for women to find college money." She thought further. "Annie, where do you see God in this?"

That spun Anika's head up. She stared at her friend, realizing Allie cared enough to figure out the right questions for her. She squeezed Allie's shoulder.

Allie laughed, raising her eyebrows. "Nailed it, did I?" They walked on in shared silence, watching the light and shadow, a red-tailed hawk circling high above, whistling. Finally, Anika responded.

"I see God here. In you. In this sunrise and that hawk up there. Between us. And in this baby that's growing in me. In Sly. In our lovemaking. It'll be all right. I know now. Hard, but all right. I gotta do it because it's just in me to do. You know?"

Allie felt apprehensive, although she knew it was Anika's choice that mattered, a journey she had to take. She smiled her agreement to stick around for her friend, no matter what. "I'm in, kid. We'll do this together too."

"You're the best."

"Annie? Ready to shift gears?"

"Sure. I'm ready." She sang a little made-up tune. "Always ready for you-u, baby. What's on your mind?"

"Sometimes I get bored with Jeff. I love him and all, but he's so—um, right wing in his politics and his religious beliefs. He's not an adventurer like I try to be, want to be. I love a challenging math problem, a mountain we haven't yet climbed. You know how I am." She paused for Anika's acknowledgment. "I mean, he's steady and good, but—you know—boring. There. I said the *b* word."

Anika waited for Allie to finish her thoughts. This was an old issue between Jeff and Allie, something big Allie had to work out in her mind. Anika knew her part was just to be the sounding board, as Allie did so well for her. No advice until asked.

"Something new happen that you're bringing it up now?" Anika pressed in.

"We got in a fight about Nixon and Kennedy's campaigns the other night. I can't believe he supports that idiot Nixon—he's *so* ignorant. How can anybody with a brain not see how promising the Kennedys are— forward-thinking, worldly, education-minded compared to the status-quo posturing of phony Nixon and his ilk. It frustrates me to listen to Jeff, like I don't even know him. Or want to. How could I love such a wrong-head I don't agree with and think of spending my whole life with him, raise kids with him?"

Anika pondered awhile, knowing her feedback was now wanted. "It's possible if you want to marry him because you love him more than politics, values. Then yes, you can do it by letting him have his views and you have yours. You know, live and let live?"

They climbed over a fallen tree on the path. Simultaneously, both paused to take a drink of water from their canteens, grinning at each other for the shared moment.

"You know, Al," Anika said, scratching her leg. "What I just said? That's just theoretical pie-in-the-sky crap. What I really *feel* is, since you asked—you're passionate about your politics, and you have a forward-thinking, adventurous spirit. Jeff is solid, decent, and not a little conservative. He gives money to the Nixon campaign because he believes in what the guy stands for. I think you hate what Nixon stands for, am I right?" She took in Allie's vigorous nodding. "So this is more than whose favorite color clashes with whose. This is core values stuff. And this is who-do-I-want-to-wake-up-to-every-livelong-day-of-my-life decision time."

"You're right. I think that's it. It would be a long haul with a man whose views I don't like or respect. What would I tell my kids when he ranted about things that are crazy to me?"

"Al, I know how important this is to you. It's good that you're naming it finally."

The two walked on in silence. Allie shook her hands vigorously as if to shake out her thoughts.

"This *is* big, isn't it, Annie? This is decision time, and I'm scared to blow this." She plopped down on a boulder, resigned to face up to this. Anika sat beside her.

"It's real big. Let's look at your options. Say you break up with Jeff. What have you lost?"

"Oh, just the only boyfriend I've ever wanted. Maybe the only one I'll ever have."

"C'mon, girl. That's bunk, and you know it. You're pretty, you're smart, you're going someplace, and you're cool. You just haven't fished in the big pool yet."

"But there's no proof that anything better can work out for me." Allie looked off at the horizon, now lit up in bright morning sun. The view was the right backdrop for her deep thoughts. She saw the scene as exaggerating her fear of the unknown—or was it new hope?

"There's no proof for any of us, my friend. And you won't know the great love I can already see for you until you get out there and find out." Anika looked deep into Allie's eyes. "You've got it, girl. You're a real star, Al. You think God doesn't want what's best for you?"

Anika's certainty was evident, convincing. It confirmed Allie's greatest hope. She was bigger than this and destined for more.

"Would you rather know now, before you have six rug rats and a husband you can't stand? Besides, he's been your *only* boyfriend. What do you and I know of the big world out there?"

"We'll have to be so careful not to repeat what's in our gene pools, hunh? You'll hold my feet to the fire if I hold yours so we can overcome the crapola?"

"Yeah, haven't we always? So our role models stink, but at least that shows us what we *don't* want for our lives. That's worth *some*thing. Our parents did *some* hard research for us!" They laughed at their similar crazy alcoholic families.

"Allie. I worry about Sly's drinking. A *lot*."

"I know. Me too."

"Let's both keep an eye on it. This is just what we're talkin' about—holding each other's feet to the fire. Actually holding Sly's feet IN the fire!" Allie grimaced.

They laughed loud again and linked their pinky fingers in a promise pact. Then back out on the trail for a leg and heart-stretching hike.

23

Sly—1958

At Westinghouse, they called him Sly Dog or just Dawg. An expediter, Sly Starner moved parts and product through the system, so he was everywhere in the factory and well known. Tall, handsome, surly, smart, Sly was the guy the men envied but dared not be. He walked the wild side, a James Dean sort. Women were drawn to his sexiness. He was aware of his power and wielded it at will. No slave to old-fashioned faithfulness, he believed his powers of seduction were God-given, a kind of compensation for not having the family advantages of the college brats in management. He believed he was smarter than most. And he knew the edge of trouble he could approach, then back off with a palms-up play of no-harm-intended.

Only one man at the plant held his respect—fifty-seven-year-old Clint Wilder, department chief and Sly's boss. Sly respected Clint for his clear intelligence, good intentions, and uncanny ability to ferret out the truth. Brooking no bullshit, Clint would watch as ambitious egos danced fast for their few moments of recognition during tedious division meetings. Then he would offer the distilled core issues and solutions that often led to quick closure. He had the reputation as the voice of reason.

Sly would climb the back stairs to Clint's office in hopes of a few moments, maybe even coffee, with this wise one every excuse he got. He wondered how his life would have been different if he'd had a father like this good man. In Sly's mind, Clint stood shoulders above the crowd.

Sly never dared speak of his great admiration—men just didn't talk such mush—but he showed it in little favors and in his tone, his respectful demeanor around Clint. Sly was a better man around Clint.

"Sit down, man. You look like you could use some coffee." Clint always read people carefully, and usually accurately. He poured a cup for his young friend, thinking how Sly reminded him of his younger, cockier self. As he handed the coffee to Sly, Clint smelled last night's beer on Sly's breath.

"Phew, man. Hittin' the bottle again last night? Or the whole brewery?"

"Yeah, I tipped a few with the guys." Defensive now, he stirred cream and sugar into his coffee. He tried shifting the blame.

"Man, it's brutal out there, Clint. Natives are restless. The sheet metal line is all messed up by that fool of a sheet metal operator, DeLauter. He backed up the whole line. They're standing around with their thumbs up their butts, talking trash to pass the time. Damn, they specialize in hiring idiots in this dump."

"Yeah, really. He's somebody's cousin's brother-in-law like half the idiots out on that floor. But, Dawg, why are you letting it get to you this time? I thought you were smarter than that." Clint leaned back in his chair, tilting his head with the squint that meant full bore attention, hands behind his head.

Sly shifted uneasily, eyes on the floor. "Aw, I don't know, guess I'm just tired of idiots." He knew better than to insult Clint's intelligence by cover-up lies. He wondered if Clint had already heard of his latest escapade with a new woman on the electrical line. He'd made a pass at her yesterday, then took her parking over the lunch break.

Clint grunted, said nothing, just watched him squirm.

"You know, Dawg, I'm not quite as dumb as I look. And I'm very fond of that beautiful woman of yours. I hope you're treating her right."

Sly shifted in his seat and cleared his throat. He feigned a coughing fit and stood up, backing out the door, mumbling his "S'cuse me."

I'm so busted. That guy sees everything. I'll have to lie low for a while.

Damn fool, Clint realized. *No idea how good he's got it. He's gonna have to lose some to find out what matters in life. Hope he doesn't fall too hard.*

24

Anika and Sly—1957

Anika's breasts were beginning to swell, her nipples turning dark, signs that meant this pregnancy was real. She and Sly were parking at their favorite Helderberg Mountain overlook with the big view of the city lights, Anika's favorite view.

"Hon, I have something to tell you." She was apprehensive about how Sly would respond. She leaned forward and rubbed her palms together, a familiar gesture that he knew meant something big. *Pay-attention time.*

"Figured. You were antsy at dinner. So—you're pregnant? Who's the father?" He nuzzled her neck.

She laughed and punched his arm muscle lightly. "Father Joe. Or maybe Father Brian. Better it be Father Brian, with his cute profile. But then again . . . Father Joe's brains would be good. But then all that hair on a little girl—can't picture that. God only knows. Could be either of them." She gave him a wry lip-twister smile.

Sly could feel the relief in her banter, belying her nervousness. This was an unknown world they'd stumbled into. He pulled her close as the truth she was not yet saying began to dawn on him.

"Holy moly, baby. You just getting around to telling me this?" He thought his heart would burst. "Oh my GOD!"

"I wanted to be sure, not just freak you out over nothin'. You're such a worrier—I guess I wanted to protect you in case it was just a late period." She pulled back her hair, then let it fall again.

"Protect me from my own baby? From my woman? Thanks anyway, hon, but I want to man up to share everything with you. You're my woman and I want to protect *you* and know everything about my baby." He ran his finger over his lips, then held it there, thinking *this is what I hoped would happen. Push me into committing to Annie and make me settle down.* But he underestimated the power of his addictive nature.

She burrowed into him, lingering sweetly in the newness of this deeper connection. He held her in long silent together love.

She pulled back a little. "I took a test at Planned Parenthood. I have an appointment with them in two weeks for a confirmation check. But this test should be reliable, they told me. And I know in my heart that this is real. My body is showing it."

"Really, baby? You're sure? This is for *real?*" He was overwhelmed with happiness, then fear, then a heavy responsibility. Then wonder. "Whoa! I'm gonna be a dad! He opened his window and yelled out to all of greater Albany, "I'm gonna be a DAAA-DD! Here we come world!"

She smiled gladly at him. This was going better then she had imagined.

"I hope it'll be healthy, you know, whole and fun and beautiful," he continued. "But if not . . . can I imagine loving this baby if it's retarded or crippled or something? Can you?" He shook that thought off as if to avoid jinxing the babe. "I know it'll be a beauty, with your looks and my brains." He shot a goofy grin at her.

She imagined with him, waving her hand slowly across the horizon to reveal the picture before them—"Your basketball buddy and my running pal"—and laughed her delight at the thought of their wonderful child.

"What's your hunch, boy or girl?" He wanted to savor and explore each part of this mystery with her, dream with her.

"You know," she said thoughtfully, "I think it's a girl. Just a hunch. We'll get to pick names for either, of course. Oh man, I'm SO excited!"

This was going to work, she believed. They would do this together. She cried tears of shared joy, of relief, of love for Sly and this mysteriously growing baby. She could build a tender nest for this new life in her womb. She was ready now.

~ ~ ~

Allie was the reluctant bridesmaid for the small family wedding in December. She saw her purpose as stalwart back-up girl. Allie saw the parallels of Sly with Anika's father that Anika's love for Sly obscured. *Both drunks, both lousy attitudes. God be with her.*

"So let's go down the damn aisle and get this over with, okay? C'mon, I'll be nice and pretend. Promise." She hugged her best pal, laughing.

The assembled family and friends smiled and said how lovely was the wedding ceremony Anika and Sally put together, and went home a little worried in their bellies.

Anika whispered before the nuptials, "For better or worse . . . promise you'll stick around, Al?" Allie nodded, with a subtle eye-rolling grin.

~   ~   ~

Six months later: "You smell like the perfume counter at Macy's," Anika observed as she climbed heavily into bed where Sly lay drinking a beer and watching TV one night. "You could at least try to be a little subtle. You bring home a disease, Dog, and I'm gone. Got that?"

How does she always know? I washed it off. She's got a nose for shit, damn her. "Well, if you must know, smarty pants, I was shopping for perfume for your birthday." He finished his beer and set the empty down on his nightstand.

"Right, Romeo. And I'm Cleopatra, queen of the Nile. *Good* night." She slid to her edge of the bed.

"Aww, baby—"

"Sly, please. Don't waste your breath trying to insult my intelligence with your bullshit. Do I really look that dumb?"

Silence. Soon the admission of his snoring.

Dear God, help me to accept this drunken, cheatin' fool. Thank You for a bit of peace of mind, and for You to talk to. There's no other way I can see to live something decent for this baby in my womb. Or, if I should leave, would You show me, please? Or how about showing me how to take him out without getting caught? Just kidding. Sort of. I know You love the fool, though I don't know how You do it. But then again, You love me, and I'm not always the coolest thing in town. So thanks.

Deep down in her heart, Anika felt God chuckle. She smiled and drifted into dreamland.

25

Carlos—1958

Carlos's real estate business prospered in his early years with the help of his cousin and mentor, Alfredo Ruiz, who took him in and taught him the tools of his trade. They made good money, brokering some lucrative deals that highlighted Carlos's sales talents. Alfredo was honest and hardworking, and genuinely interested in promoting Carlos for good business and family relations. The family welcomed Sally and the children into their fold with gusto.

"You got th' gift o' gab, Carlos, me man. Make a nice living for your family," Alfredo told him when they made a big sale. "Keep that mouth of yours working. Little more experience and you'll do fine. Stick wi' me, man. Your family will help you. Oh, and easy on the drinkin'."

As the Spanish community expanded with work-seeking Latin American immigrants, Carlos and Alfredo rode the first wave as the only viable Spanish-speaking realtors in the Albany district for a time. Carlos was ambitious, smart, and attractive. He had a good woman, nice kids, and work that flowed in; he believed he had it all. And as he grew cocky with success, his drinking progressed.

It began in the service. Drinking seemed to him the way to fit in, the reward for the hard lonely days of army life. Liquor and drugs flowed easy. When his first child died mysteriously in her crib, Carlos the soldier blamed himself for not being able to protect his baby from some unknown disaster. Drinking took the edge off the pain and gave him the illusion of control.

His mother was kind and solicitous with him and Sally through the painful hours, quietly making meals and cleaning, helping Sally organize the baby's funeral. She welcomed friends and family to allow everyone to grieve. Sally's mother showed up and sat quietly with visitors, ran errands, and brought fresh flowers.

Carlos's father crossed his arms and sat, saying little to anyone. "When ees las' time you take Diana to baby doctor?" his father asked hoarsely, looking at no one.

"She had her last checkup two weeks ago, Pop. Right, honey?" Carlos responded warily. He knew well his father's blaming ways.

"Yes, just ten days, actually. She was perfect on the growth charts and gaining weight right on time. The pediatrician said, 'Fine healthy girl you have, Mrs. Mendoza. Whatever you're feeding her, keep it up.' He said it was sudden infant crib death which they don't know much about or why it happens."

Sally welled up again with tears she felt would never dry up. She knew her father-in-law had to blame something for Diana's death, that he was searching for answers nobody had. She knew to allow him to have his own way of grieving, to not take it personally. She caught Carlos's eye on her and received his supportive nod. He moved close to her and put a protective arm around her, glaring defiantly at his father, daring him to judge Sally. His father retreated into staring at the floor in silence.

"Son of a bitch never loved us like he loved Diana," Carlos whispered to Sally, who turned into him and held on. "He better *never* say anything nasty about this." Carlos ramped up his drinking from that time on. Bitter disappointment and self-blame gave him the excuse.

Carlos's mother watched them all sadly, grieving in her heart for them. She knew Carlos as her eldest had always felt responsible for his siblings, taking their accidents or struggles to heart. She willed herself to simply be kind so they could grieve as they needed. Catholic faith was her comfort in terrible times like this. She didn't ask why this had happened. She cleaned up after everyone and patted their shoulders, and handed out the Kleenex. *What would Mary do?* she thought in her heart.

~   ~   ~

One stormy afternoon in October, Carlos wove his way home from the bar, stiff drunk. He slowed for a stoplight. A pick-up truck came up from behind too fast to stop on the wet road. "Oh shit," he slurred, fumbling with the gearshift but too impaired to get out of the way in time. It rammed Carlos's sedan into the middle of the intersection as a garbage truck rumbled through, mangling his car, killing him instantly.

Sally had expected something like this for a long time. She hated admitting to herself how greatly relieved she felt, mixed with deep sadness for the misery of his chosen life. She sat with her somber children in the second row at the funeral service. The girls' faces were open books as many feelings and memories washed their way out with tears. Peter's face was a stone mask. He barely managed to sit there.

Father Joe, now a senior priest in a large church across town, officiated, his own emotions doing battle in his heart as he offered the consolations of his calling. Father Brian had offered to assist him in the service, knowing how close he was to this family. Father Joe was grateful to have his support; this would be a tough one. He was most concerned about Peter, who was now twenty-two, getting ready to launch his life, still in college, living at home.

Peter never cried. He closed his arms like his grandfather and held it all in.

Father Joe had arranged to meet Peter on the old basketball court after the service. The priest was now a graying forty years, a little paunchy, wrinkles creasing his kind brown eyes. He shot the ball hard at Peter, whose face was a stiff angry mask. Peter dribbled thoughtfully for a while, glad to have his mentor's companionship at such an intense time.

"Okay, buddy. It's over. How are you gonna get on with *your* life now?" Father Joe was direct—*get to work, boy. Time to move on.*

Peter felt a tiny space shift in his heart. He poised the ball on his fingertips a minute as his feelings gathered.

"First, I'm gonna kill the son of a bitch again. Then a-GAIN. SON of a bitch!" He slammed the ball as hard as he could against the wall. "God—I hated him!" Father Joe threw him back the ball. Peter slammed it viciously again and again. He felt his rage could never spend itself. It was a volcano, a molten fire from the core of his heart. Huge.

Over and over, Peter slammed the ball against the wall with all his might. Father Joe waited, praying for his young friend.

Father, I know you love my young pal, and that You've watched over him while that nutcase beat on him all those years out of his own self-loathing. Hold him in your big warm loving embrace as only You can. Break this damned chain of drunken insanity in THIS generation. Thank You! And that service was the damnedest farce I ever faked my way through. Yeah. I admit it. I hated him. How could I not? So THANK You for helping me at least go through the motions civilly.

Feeling Father Joe's genuine love, the dam broke and the tears came. *Finally.* Father Joe walked over to hug him. Peter wailed. "Oh *God!*" he yelled. Father Joe held him until his crying subsided.

"What would I do without you, you old goat? See what you made me do?" Peter snuffled into Father Joe's shoulder. "Like when I was a kid."

"Sweet Jesus Malone, boy! I'd say it's about time you laid this burden down." Father Joe threw back his head and grinned. "C'mon, my bawling reject . . . what're you waiting for? Shoot that thang!"

26

Sally—November 1958

Sally did what she had to do. She buried Carlos, took account of their dismal finances, and went shopping. Carlos's drinking had taken its toll. Little savings were left, a few thousand. His life insurance paid little more than burial expenses, creditors, and mortgage arrears.

Father Joe looked in on her one afternoon and laughed his appreciation of her new look of freedom from bondage. Her cheeks were rosier, her head higher, her walk lighter. "Classy broad! Where'd you come from?" Mimicking the street talk of his Boston home turf, he added, "Who knew you were such a good looker wit' chur wild self?"

She hugged him hard in appreciation of his priceless support through the tough years and their honest friendship. "I'm off to an Al-Anon meeting tonight, so somebody else is gonna have to feed you." She knew well that her good home cooking had nourished him over the years, balancing the give-and-take a little. "What would Peter and I ever have done without you?"

"Have a fuller refrigerator?" Father Joe waved his characteristic off-hand farewell as he walked down her driveway.

That man is higher powered indeed, she thought—a true gift in their lives.

~   ~   ~

Sally found a secretarial job at a lawyer's office downtown, close enough to walk to work on fine days. She slowly felt her way into her new single working life. She had good people instincts, a quick mind, the determination to learn, and the faith of a survivor.

Waiting for their Al-Anon meeting to start one night, Sally told Cass, "I can get used to having a regular paycheck. With Peter and Anika pretty self-sufficient, I feel like a free new being. Kinda weird and kinda wonderful. Al-Anon is helping me learn to live in today and leave the past behind. Thank you for dragging me here." She winked.

"You're a trooper, Mom. You're just the sort of open-minded soul who understands how freeing this program truly is." Cass turned to welcome a new arrival. Then, quietly, "Mom—I've been thinking. Maybe it's time to think about your social life. You've still got great legs and a killer smile, not to mention a wonderful personality, wisdom, fine cooking. How about it? You still in the running?"

"Maybe I'm not all dried up yet, you're saying? We'll see. I will admit only to you that there's a lawyer in my office I have my eye on. Don't know if he's married, though he doesn't wear a wedding ring. I'm paying attention, huzzy that I am." She laughed at her new bolder, more courageous self.

Not long after, Sally was headed out of the office to a noon Al-Anon meeting she'd heard about. Lots of quality recovery there she should check out, an Al-Anon friend had said. She bumped into that interesting lawyer on the elevator. She knew his name was Andrew Thatcher.

"Going out to lunch, pretty lady?" he asked a bit diffidently. He recognized her from his partner's office staff.

"Actually, I'm going to a twelve-step meeting on Pearl Street," she said, a little embarrassed to confess.

"Al-Anon or AA?" he asked with interest. "Oh, I'm sorry, I'm Andrew. I work with Tony."

"Hi, Andrew. I'm Sally. You're Tony's partner, yes?" She held out her hand. She liked his strong grip. "I'm going to Al-Anon. Do you know something about twelve-step programs?"

"Too much!" he joked. "Actually, that's where I'm headed, to AA. Mind if I tag along?"

"Not at all. Pleased to have your company. I'm new to this meeting. Maybe you can show me where it meets."

"Glad to have the company." He smiled full into her face. "So, Sally, I've been hearing about what a fine hire you've been for Tony." His eyes crinkled at the corners with crow's feet, a feature she'd always liked. She noticed his wavy gray hair and startling blue eyes, even more enticing up close. She hoped he wouldn't notice she was blushing, schoolgirl-shy. *He has to be married; he's too good-looking and nice not to be.*

They walked the two blocks in easy chatter, though her nervous heart was pounding. *I feel like a goose,* she chided herself. *Way too old to be nervous as a thirteen-year-old with this man I don't even know.*

"Here we are," he said as he opened the heavy glass door for her. "Your meeting is on the second floor, first door to the right of the stairs. Ours is down the hall here. Catch up with you in an hour?"

"Okay, great, thanks," she murmured. *This is all too much—but I like it,* she admitted. *Maybe I'm not such a has-been after all. He seems sincere. What would it be like to make friends with a decent recovering man?*

She found the people at the meeting to be an older group with a lot of years in the program. The one man among the ladies spoke philosophically about his deceased Irish alcoholic wife, which put Sally at ease. He had had the same kind of experience living with a drunken spouse as she had. Raising kids mostly alone, fearful of his wife's effect on the kids. And he had to work to earn their keep, too.

"Never knew what I was comin' home to—house on fire, kids locked in a closet, the postman being mauled by the dog. Yup. They all happened, but I might have the order a little befuddled." Everybody laughed, and some identified in, nodding.

She approached him after the meeting. "Thanks for your sharing. I related to everything you said."

"Yes, I saw the understanding in your face as I was sharing. Thanks for coming. It helps lighten my load to talk with others who've been there and can relate. Please come back. I need people like you who get it. Helps me know I wasn't alone with this killer disease."

She smiled shyly and thanked him, then left to meet Andrew. He looked more relaxed, a fresh sparkle in his eyes. She wondered if she looked different to him than before her meeting too.

"Great meeting!" he said. "The speaker told a powerful, really funny story. How was yours? From the look of you, it was a good one."

So it does *show,* she thought. *Guess my meeting left me sparkling too.*

"It was really good," she said grinning "Those folks are so wise and real. I'm getting it that others can actually relate to my crazy life by virtue of their own! One man sounded like he had lived my story—it was amazing. His wife died of the disease too."

"Yeah, that's the deal. We're all nuts. It's said that we're all here because we're not all there!"

"Ain't *that* the truth!" Sally laughed loud at that. Then, surprised, she said, "Funny how great it is to laugh about it all—feels so healing somehow."

"It is. I never thought I'd EVER laugh at this stinkin' disease."

This guy is real, she thought. *He laughs easily and honestly. Oh—humility! If this is what recovering alcoholics are like, deal me in.*

They walked on, comfortably side by side in their own thoughts.

His next words warmed her heart. "Maybe you'll go back next week then, Sally? Want to walk over there again with me?"

"You bet. Thanks, that would be nice," she answered enthusiastically. "I feel kind of like the new kid on the playground, so it's good to have company."

"My wife died four years ago. We used to drink together, and it got her quicker than me—maybe her Irish blood! And that's what got me sober. Finally." He chuckled and half turned toward her. "I'm sort of like the guy at your meeting but likely more complicit. Less saintly."

"I'm sorry," she said sincerely. "That must have been so hard."

"You remarried?" he asked hesitantly, glancing sidelong at her ring finger. She still wore her wedding ring out of habit.

"No, I just wear my ring still. Carlos died in a car wreck just a year ago, nearly two actually," she said reflectively. "There've been many changes since then. My kids are pretty much grown, so I have a lot of new freedom. It's a bit scary. But I'm finding some new fun. The job has gotten me out into a whole new world. And Al-Anon too . . ." She raised her eyebrows to Andrew.

"Yeah, I faced a whole bunch of new things when Sheila died, things I'd taken for granted, things that scared me silly at first but now seem pretty doable. Like cooking a decent meal. And, oh yeah, feelings—God forbid a man should catch a feeling!"

He laughed at himself, a sign Sally liked. Carlos could never laugh at himself, she remembered bitterly. He'd make fun of others but could never take a joke or look at himself with any real honesty. Gradually, the booze choked out everything good in him.

They arrived back at the office building. In the elevator, Andrew looked hopefully at Sally. "Hey, Sally, I don't mean to rush you, but is there any chance I could take you to dinner some night? Sounds like we might offer each other some company."

"That would suit me fine." She smiled quickly, thinking of any plans for the weekend. "I'm free this Saturday." *No sense being coy with this sharp guy. Be direct. Go for what you want. Because what do you have to lose but your fear?*

"Perfect! Pick you up at six—oh, you'll have to tell me where."

"127 Chestnut Street, a yellow brick with blue shutters. On the left going south."

"I'll be the guy with the old gray sweater and jeans, if casual suits your fancy."

"Lovely. I look forward to it."

Sally walked with winged feet to her office. She couldn't believe he had asked her out already.

Andrew whistled down the hall. *This is one sweet gal, I can tell. Higher Power, help me mind my p's and q's so I don't run her off before I even know her. Thank You for my blessed sobriety. Here we go! I feel ready, thanks to You and sobriety.*

Their first date was a relaxed pleasure. Andrew chose a renovated ferryboat restaurant for its private candlelit ambiance. He was at ease in his favorite gray sweater and jeans. Sally thought him exquisite-looking. She'd taken his hint and dressed casually in a black sweater and slacks. *Stunning,* he thought.

"Thank you for sharing your evening with me, Sally. This is a great pleasure for me. I work too much and don't get out to play nearly enough. Especially with a woman way too beautiful for the likes of me. So thanks. This is wonderful." He leaned forward, both hands on the table edge, smiling at her, his face sincere, almost childlike.

Sally battled fear and delight and couldn't tell which was winning. She smiled warmly back at him. "Yes. Me too. This is lovely. Been a long time since I had a wonderful evening out with a good man. And a recovering one at that. Thank *you*, Andrew. I love this place. I've seen it before and wanted to come in but never had the chance." She relaxed a little, warmed by the glow of candlelight and his good company, the gentle rocking of the boat on the river. They sipped ginger ales.

As they lingered over their meals, they shared some stories, laughing at some highlights and lowlights. Sally soon saw she could talk to him about anything and everything.

"When did you get into AA, if I'm not being nosy?" she asked.

"Boy, do I remember *that* miserable day. Sheila had died about a year back, liver failure. Watching her deteriorate was the hardest thing I'd ever gone through. She was a wonderful mother and wife in so many ways, but once she started drinking, mostly to keep me company, she went downhill fast. Her dad was a drunk. I think watching him disintegrate gave her an excuse to drink. Seemed like once she had the bit in her teeth, she was off and running." He wiped his mouth with his napkin, then dabbed at his eyes. "Wow, I didn't know there were still tears *in* me!" He laughed, embarrassed.

She nodded in simple understanding, glad he was comfortable enough to be candid with her. Holding up a forkful of chicken cordon bleu, Sally made an "mmm" sound. He read the pleasure on her face and felt happier than he had in years. He liked that she didn't try to fix his tears, just accepted him as he was.

"Are you always this easy to be with, Miss Sally? Or are you a real good character actress, pulling this old fool's leg?" He took a drink of water, looked mock-intense in his best courtroom tactics. "Am I going to wake from this fantasy?" He cocked his head, smiling, loving this comfortable banter.

She chuckled. "I'm just having a wonderful evening with an honest man—one who actually *shares* ordinary human feelings like grief, and the terrible loss of a beloved wife. How refreshing." She reached for his hand. They touched hearts and hands for a moment.

A year later, they wed in a warm family ceremony at Andrew's home, now theirs to share. Father Joe led the celebration, decked out in a fresh robe with a bright scarlet surplice.

"Hallelujah! is all I can say," Father Joe boomed as the ceremony rounded up.

At the reception following, Sally took Cass aside and nodded over at Andrew's son, Zack, a recovering alcoholic, a mechanic, divorced with two kids, living in Lennox, Massachusetts. "A sweet guy, honey. I'd like you to meet him. His dad's real proud of him."

"Sure, Mom. I've been checking him out. Hunk like his dad, hunh?" She jerked her eyebrows up and down a couple of times. "Ain't recovering families just all that AND apple pie a la mode?"

Sally introduced Zack and Cass, then stepped back to see if the spark would catch. Zack's two kids, Kiera and Tim, circled in, instantly alert.

"What would you think of a match between Zack and Cassandra, honey?" she asked Andrew as she returned to him with a sly grin.

"Whoa! Aren't you a slick one. Actually, I don't know if he's ready—he's not even divorced yet and in AA for what, a year and a half?"

"We'll see. They do look good together, though, don't you think? Be still, my heart!"

Andrew put his arm around his bride and squeezed. "I'd hate to be up against you in court. Good footwork, slick."

27

Zack—October 1960

Cassandra and Zack left the wedding reception to get coffee at Cass's favorite coffee spot. *Striking chick with her red curls and her quick mind,* Zack thought. She found him rugged, thoughtful. It was the start of an easy minds' meeting. They had enough in common besides their looks to attract each other, as her mother had foreseen. Both were between relationships.

"Nice of the groom to keep an eye on your kids so we could step out, busy as he is," she said. "We'd better watch the time so we don't impose too much." She noted the time, then looked at the menu and grew thoughtful. "He seems like an aces grandpa, yes? Really loves the kids, and they seem to adore him?"

Zack nodded. "Yes, he's wonderful with them. Gives them lots of attention without spoiling them. And they like your mom so far."

"Nice. But isn't this just a little incestuous, having coffee with step-kin?" Cass winked.

"Yeah, I think *so.* I hear it's illegal to drink coffee with your step-kin in Alaska and West Virginia." Zack grimaced. He hoped her insides matched her outsides. He'd been burned by an early sobriety relationship and learned the lessons of "think" and "easy does it," as the AA slogans read, painfully.

Cass was gun-shy too. Al-Anon was teaching her where she'd faltered in previous relationships and why she'd unconsciously chosen repeats of her father. "The family disease," Al-Anon called it. Everyone is affected. She felt a bit clearer about making healthy choices now. She wondered if Zack was yet another test or a new friend in the family.

"Tell me your story and take your time," she said, hands folded under her chin.

"All right then, Miss Cassandra. Let's see—I'm Dad's oldest and best." He grinned and shook his head a little. "Except I caught his disease and I lost everything—wife, kids, a decent career in car sales. Couldn't see my drinking was causing everything nasty that was happening. When I hit bottom, I was finally ready to go with Dad to an AA meeting, seeing what it did for him. He was a loony son of a gun when I was growing up, and AA turned him around like a miracle cure. I love the hell outa him now, but growing up was no picnic. Things went downhill fast when us kids were pretty independent and Mom started drinking with him."

Zack shifted in his seat and brushed his longish dark wavy hair back. Cass noticed his deep-set blue eyes, his strong chin.

"And you, lady? What's your story? What line of work are you in?" he asked.

"Well—where to begin?" Cass smoothed a wrinkle in her navy dress and wrapped her fingers around her coffee mug. "I'm a buyer for Sears now. I just got promoted. Lots of travel, which I like. Meeting new people, shopping and getting paid for it. Pretty cushy work if you can get it." She took a sip of coffee. Her expression turned pensive.

"My dad was a drunk too, Latino, and mean as a snake—not nice like Andrew, at least what I've seen of him so far. Mom's a free soul now, and it's well deserved for putting up with Dad all those years and holding the family together. I give her all the credit for my fleeting sanity." She twinkled with a gentle humility that he found disarming.

Cass leaned back in her booth seat. "Father Joe, who did the wedding ceremony? He's been a good family friend for maybe fifteen, sixteen years. He's the one who finally pointed me in the direction of Al-Anon after I'd done the relationship crazy-dance a few times. Higher Power gave me a friend at work, my roommate, Angie, who took me to my first meeting, and I knew I was in." She smiled gratefully. "And Mom came too when she saw how much it was helping me. And here we are making new lives out of the ashes of our 'research.' I'm so grateful for Mom, and we're *all* glad for Andrew being with Mom. Although Pete . . ."

Cassandra crossed her legs and took a sip of coffee. "Yuck. Cold." She shook her head and chuckled a little to soften her fussiness.

Zack looked for the waitress and held up two fingers for two fresh coffees. "Want some pie? Are they homemade?"

"You bet. They have great homemade pastries. That's why Mom and I love this place. Especially their blueberry and pecan pies."

"So . . . you were saying about Pete? He seems a little hard to get to know, but interesting. Sharp."

She sat staring out the window for a long moment, then turned to him with a direct gaze. *Might as well shoot the moon from the outset. He'll find out the truth about us soon enough anyway.*

"Peter was Dad's punching bag. He could never do anything right. It was merciless." She wiped her lips with her napkin. She sat still, looking at her hands. Zack waited. The waitress put down two generous pieces of pecan pie a la mode. Zack nodded to her.

"He's a great guy, actually. Smart and funny, a great mechanic. Wants to be a writer."

Zack reached across the table to give her hand a quick encouraging squeeze.

Cass felt a thrill in her gut at his touch. She jerked her head a little and smiled at him, collecting herself. "I guess the reason I'm telling you this is— now that we're family—the other night, Annie was at Mom's helping plan the wedding, and Pete was upstairs in his room studying. Annie was sticking out to here, you know?" she said, holding her hands out in front in a circle. "All at once the door flew open, and in blew Sly—and I do mean *blew*—three sheets to the wind and cussing a blue streak. Mom said everybody froze." She sipped her coffee.

"'Where the hell you been, Anika? I've been frantic. No dinner, no note.' Sly looked around the table angrily. Mom said he looked like a caged animal. Annie struggled to her feet and said, 'Sly. I told you this morning I was coming over tonight to help Mom with the wedding.' About that time, Pete came flyin' down the stairs. He walked up to Sly and stood toe to toe, breathing fire. Sly faced off with him, then turned on his heel, slamming the door hard on his way out. Everybody just sat there. Pete went back upstairs. Wasn't much to say. Anika apologized for Sly, and they all just sat there for a minute." Cass picked up her water for a taste.

"Then Mom in her infinite wisdom told Anika that Al-Anon was helping her deal with her stuff about Dad's drinking, and that she'd love to take Annie to a meeting if she ever wanted. Annie cried a little, then suggested they get back on track, which they did. Andrew held his peace, Mom said. She sure loves your dad, Zack. He's great. And she's so appreciative after the hell Dad made of her life."

She took a bite of pie. "Now that's *pie*, right?" toasting its goodness with a flourish of her fork.

Zack scratched his eyebrow. "Yeah, this is pecan *pie* all right, missy," waving his fork like a baton. And, Cass . . . this feels good—this conversation. I feel like I've found a new friend in the family. I get what you're saying about

Pete. It's this way in alcoholic families, and it's tough, and embarrassing. But there it is."

Cass flashed a full eyebrow-wiggling smile at him. "Yep. Thanks for your understanding. I get the feeling I've just found a friend in the family too, Mr. Zack. Maybe West Virginny is wrong."

28

September 1957

Allie's boyfriend, Jeff, joined the Republican students' alliance at Rensselaer Polytechnic Institute in Troy, New York, as soon as he got to college. That did it for Allie. She knew she had been hanging on by a thread, and so did Jeff. Their relationship ended naturally, so they stayed friends, which Allie liked because she was very fond of him and his family. "He makes a better friend than boyfriend," she told Anika.

"You guys had a good run, girl. You'll always love Jeff—and so will I, for that matter. He's a good guy. He's just not for you. Too conservative, too dry, too engineer-y. You need more spark. You *are* more spark."

"You named it, Annie, as usual. Thanks for seeing me so well, pal."

"That'll cost you fifty dollars in shrink's fees."

"You work cheap. Put it on my tab." Allie smiled and marked in the air with her pointer finger.

Allie loved math. She saw the beauty and order of the universe in terms of equations, and loved nothing better than opening its mysteries, making sense out of chaos. She worked equations in her head the way Anika thought about what made people tick, enjoying the process of thinking, analyzing. Allie's aunt, who had raised her, saw she was a math whiz and encouraged her by sending her to classes and competitions wherever she could find them all through high school.

"We have to feed that hungry brain of yours, girl," she declared to Allie. "Too good to waste." After Allie and Jeff broke up, her wise aunt went on high speed to find math events to help Allie get refocused.

"Look here, Al. Union College is having a symposium for talented college kids. It seems like kind of a prep course for transfer into Union's math department. Do you want to check it out?"

"Yeah, sure, Aunty. Thanks—it looks interesting. I'll give them a call. Uh-m, you folks wouldn't mind if I don't work this summer?"

"Your education comes first to us, Al. You know that. We work, you study." She patted Allie's shoulder affectionately as she passed by her chair. "Oh, I forgot, would you like to have Father Cousin Joe—that's what you call him now?—over for dinner one night this week? He always asks for you so I told him we'd like to have him over soon."

Allie nodded emphatically to dinner with Father Joe. She applied for the Union symposium and was accepted. She loved the challenge and the visiting London School of Economics professor. It was there her thirsty mind opened to possibilities she'd only imagined before. She came to realize that she thought in equations, even dreamed them, and realized that not everyone saw the world thus—it was *her* gift.

"Annie, this is it! I've found what I can sink my teeth into for the career of my life! Wow, this is fun. And my professor thinks I can go far. He is encouraging me to transfer to Union for its good math program. And Aunty thinks I should go. What think you, pal?"

"Allie, I'm thrilled and a wee bit jealous that you're finding your gift and you're so great at it. Actually I'm more happy for you than jealous. It's great to watch you so excited about something, It gives me goose bumps, and sets the bar high for me to find that fire too."

"With your great listening gift and your analyzing mind? You'll find your way if you just believe in yourself and keep feeding that dream in your heart, girl." Allie held her friend's face in her hands and looked deep in her eyes. "You've got the goods, girl. The way will open."

Anika hugged her hard. "Where would I be without you?"

"Maybe you'll amount to something after all." Allie laughed the witchy laugh that cracked Anika up. "Hey—let's take a walk over to Father Joe's, want to?" Allie had struck up a new kind of kinship with her second cousin, finding him to be fun as well as profoundly spiritual, not "churchy" at all. She was intrigued by him as mentor.

"God's the fun in it all, Allie-girl," Father Joe said with a wink one day she'd run by his parish house. "Give Him a whirl and see if I'm lying. Better than chocolate, I'm tellin' you."

"Where do you start, Father Joe? I believe you but I don't know how." Allie stood on one leg, held her foot and stretched her other leg, then switched legs, her muscles wanting stretching.

"Just ask Him. Just invite Him in, like 'Help!' then jump back and watch. It's real simple. He wants you and loves you more than you can even imagine. He'll come to you where you are and make you know. I can't explain it—it's a mystery, and it's amazing, and it always works, somehow, sometime. *His* timing."

"Well, okay. I can do that, since you make it sound simple. If He can use the likes of you . . ." She grinned at her beloved cousin, knowing he loved to be teased as much as he loved dishing it out.

He playfully punched her arm muscle, then pulled her into a hug. He loved nothing more than sharing his love of God with those he cared about. Allie felt that deep love as he held her out in front of him, holding her shoulders, those kind eyes beaming at her.

"Hey, cuz?" Suddenly shy, a bit overwhelmed, she stammered, "M-maybe this is more caught than taught—I feel the Big Love you talk about coming through your hug. Does that make any sense?"

He threw his head back with a laugh. "You bet it does, Allie-girl! You *bet* it does. It's just that simple."

29

Recovery

Anika and Allie headed off to an Al-Anon meeting one cold damp Tuesday night in December, having researched it with Father Joe to find a good meeting. He knew a parishioner who made this his home group, said it saved his life. Father Joe asked him to look out for them.

"There's a blonde and a pregnant brunette, about twenty-two, coming to your Tuesday meeting. Would you welcome them? They're sweethearts, sharp chicks, friends of mine. The blonde is my cousin, Allie."

"You bet, Father. That's our business, welcoming family and friends of alcoholics. I'll introduce them around."

"Well, all right then. Here's your chance to reach out to two good gals and watch God go to work. You won't regret it, Reds. God's got His—no, HER—hands on them. There, I said it. Now don't let that get out or I'll be ex-communicated!" he said, laughing out loud, making Reds laugh with him.

Anika and Allie sat close to the door, looking around the room a little apprehensively for anyone they knew. Father Joe's friend Reds walked up to them, holding out his hands.

"You Father Joe's friends? Welcome to our humble rooms. If you want to talk after the meeting or join us for coffee at the Perk afterwards, just let me know." He held each of their hands in his and looked warmly at them. "So glad you came—it takes guts to show up here. Especially on a night like this." He threw back his head and laughed heartily.

Anika said, "You got that right. Scary. But we've heard so much good about Al-Anon from my mom and sister. Thanks for the warm welcome,

Reds." To Allie she later whispered, "This guy's either crazy or at peace in himself. That laugh . . ."

"Yeah *baby*. Let's stick around to find out. And what if one of my colleagues shows up? I'll crawl under my chair and out the door, is what."

The chairperson opened the meeting, asked if there were any newcomers, and warmly welcomed them. Anika and Allie relaxed a few degrees, especially when they saw no one they knew.

When the chairperson asked if there was anything from the Al-Anon literature anyone wanted to hear or read, Reds read from a book he held up called *Courage to Change*. The Fourth Step reading was about self-esteem— the ability to see ourselves as we really are, all the good and all the challenges, and the commitment to become all we can be. Anika nodded to Allie understandingly twice during the reading. Allie nodded back.

After the meeting, they went to the Perk with Reds and a few others, curious about how this program worked. Reds asked Allie what she thought so far.

"Looks like it takes a lot of courage to do what you folks are doing," she responded sincerely. "I felt intrigued—especially when I didn't see anybody I knew, thank God."

"Yeah, it does take a lot of courage to show up at your first meeting—and your second, and twelfth, and then somewhere it starts getting easier!" He threw back his head with that vigorous laugh again.

Allie decided he was okay, that his laugh was genuine.

"You seem like what the reading said—humble, comfortable in your skin. Did you learn that in Al-Anon or were you born that way?" Allie asked in her refreshingly direct way.

"I had no clue who I was when I came into Al-Anon, Allie. I was walking around in a self-loathing fog. I tried to control everything and everybody. I grew up in a chaotic alcoholic family, trying to please everybody just to survive. I've had a lot of uphill climbing to do in these rooms, lots of listening, lots of butt-kicking by my sponsor." He let out a guffaw of remembering that made Allie choke on her coffee and spit it out.

"Oh, I'm so sorry," he said, offering her a napkin. "Never could hold this laugh in. Better let you wipe that coffee off your own front or you'll think me *really* bold and nasty. Here, take some water."

Allie wiped the coffee off her chin and her sweater with a shrug. "No problem—this is an old rag. But I'll know not to sit beside you when I have coffee." She grimaced a teasing grin.

He chuckled. "Hope I won't drive you away, Allie, and you too, Anika. Father Joe said you two were good friends of his, really sharp young women. I see what he means."

Anika felt connected to this group already. "Thanks for your friendly welcome, Reds. It means a lot to both of us, makes it so much easier to come back. I want to, Allie. Do you, so far?" Allie nodded.

Anika thought for a minute. "Reds, did I hear right, that alcoholism is an actual disease? Like cancer? That means my husband, Sly, has . . . a syndrome? He's not just a selfish jerk who willfully drinks and ruins everything? And my father too? This is a revelation to me. It seems you're calling it a compulsion that they didn't choose to have, but they can learn to control? Is that it?"

"That's it, Anika. It's a brain chemistry compulsion. An alcoholic tastes his or her first beer and wants the whole case. You and I can take it or leave it, but the alcoholic has this brain chemical called THIQ—actually a big unpronounceable word called tetrahydroisoquinoline—that creates the compulsion to drink, no matter how it's destroying his life or his loved ones' lives. He denies the results of drinking—that's part of the disease. He has to want to quit BAD to fight it, and that usually takes some 'research,' meaning he or she has to hit their particular bottom, which is different for everyone." He sipped his coffee thoughtfully, watching them.

Both women stared at him, nodding with new understanding.

"Annie, that's a tough concept but it makes sense. I think I can learn a lot here." Allie saw Anika light up with hope. "What did Sly say when you told him you were coming here—or did you?"

"I told him you and I were going to a fitness lecture. Hard enough to get out of the house without dropping the bomb of Al-Anon. I'll have to take this slow and easy. But I like this. It makes sense. And he'll be glad when he sees I'm not gonna murder him in his sleep. Not tonight anyway."

"Well, there's that. Survival of all his parts." Allie chuckled. "Lucky for a day." She mimicked cutting off his head, then snipping off another body part with scissors. They both broke out in riotous laughter. Reds joined in. "Now I see what Father Joe was trying to tell me. You two are a hootenany!"

30

Miz Marymoll—May 1961

Miz Marymoll called Anika early one bright Saturday morning. Anika reached for the phone on the nightstand sleepily. Sly muttered in his sleep, yawned and turned on his side toward her.

Marymoll bubbled, "Oh, did I wake ye? I don't believe I called ye so early! So how's me gurrl? Any chance ye c'n come fer a little cinnamon roll I made fer ye?"

"Oh, Miz Marymoll, you are so sweet," she murmured drowsily, tipping the clock toward the light. Eight thirty. Decent hour for a call.

"We must be sleepin' in. You said your amazing cinnamon rolls? How's ten o'clock sound? You need anything I can get you on the way?"

"Jes' bring yerself, dear. I think I got ev'r'thing. I can't wait t' see how ye're blossomin'. Ya feelin' okay?"

"Yeah, I'm fat and sassy, Honey. I'll be over shortly then. Love you."

Sly reached out to stroke her cheek, adoring her kind ways.

Anika turned to him smiling. "That dear old soul," she said, brushing Sly's hair back from his face. "She keeps me on track more than she could possibly know. She just kinda reaches down into my heart, you know? And plucks my heart strings. God, I really *love* her. She loves me without expecting anything in return."

Sly pulled her tight to him. "Like you do to me," he whispered. He felt luckier than he deserved to have landed such a sweetheart, pretty and bright and caring. And she loved him, he could feel it. He wondered how long they were allowed to have sex into this pregnancy. That thought spurred a testosterone flush.

As Anika reached her orgasm, she felt the baby stiffen into a tight little ball in her womb. She knew it would be soon. She felt her body making ready for its delivery. She wondered about all these new things and knew she was experiencing something truly amazing.

"Sly. This is the most incredible thing. The baby tightened itself into a hard little ball when I came. What do you suppose that's all about?" She wanted so much to bond with him at this sacred time, hoping he could get it though it wasn't happening in his body. He rolled away and lit a cigarette.

"I know you aren't living this amazing process, Hon, but can you understand? Your child getting ready to come into this world?" She took his hand and put it on her belly. "Feel it?" He paused there, concentrating. His eyes grew wide and he breathed, "Wow. I *do* feel it. Wo."

He saw she wanted him here with her so he tried. "Damn, Honey, I don't know, I've never been there. Guys don't know this stuff. Can you ask your mother or Miz Marymoll?" He wanted to understand, yet felt helpless in the mystery. He knew she'd give him the benefit of the doubt, that she'd settle for a decent try. She always did.

She made a face at him and went to the bathroom to wash off.

Later with Marymoll, she spoke her puzzlement. "Why can't he just hold me, listen to me, Miz Marymoll? Why don't men get it? What's so hard to understand about us and our feelings? *You* get it. Right away and easily."

"Well now, darlin', y'er askin' a tough one there. I've seen men like that, jes' didn't get outa theirselves long enough ta listen t' their women. Must be lonely fer 'em. Think he might get it if ye kinda friendly persuaded 'im? Ye know how women do that kinda gentle-like? Jes' before the baseball bat hits 'em?"

Anika burst out laughing. "Yeah, Miz Marymoll, like my mom did with Dad. Never saw it work much, though. Hard head. But what about *my* feelings? Do I count? Does his own baby count?"

"Ye sure do count t' Gawd, m' darlin' gurl. An' Sly loves ye, ye know he does. But he's kinda shy in th' listenin' department, ya know?" She reached over to softly caress Anika's shoulder.

Anika loved that Miz Marymoll didn't excuse him nor try to fix things, just listened and tried to meet her wherever she was. It was the perfect way through tight places. She wondered if she could ever learn to be wise like that.

"Miz Marymoll, how can ever learn to be wise like you and Mom? Do I just hang in and try? Mom says I just gotta keep growing, that we never get done. But I gotta tell him, right? That's the right thing?"

"Yeah, Honey, you got the right t' be heard, and ya gotta set yer marriage straight or it'll be wrong 'fore ya even get this babe outa ye!" She laughed her warm honey-coated laughter that always softened Anika's fears a little.

"Okay, Marymoll. Thanks that you never make me feel like I don't matter, that I always have to sacrifice for somebody else. My mom confused me sometimes. I couldn't tell if she was strong or weak when she let my dad bully everybody, Peter especially. But she did have her limits—she just said it kinda softly. Sometimes I wish she'd showed me how to knock his head off with that baseball bat but not get caught!"

"Yeah, baby, I believe she struggled with that too. The old question of when t' hold 'em, when t' fold 'em, like my Seamus use'ta say 'bout his poker hands."

"These are your best cinnamon rolls *ever*. You're such a treasure." Anika licked the cinnamon off her fingers, purring her contentment.

31

Birthing—June 1961

On a June morning, Anika awoke with contraction pains at 4:12 a.m. She woke Sly and started timing her contractions. When they were four minutes apart, Sly sped to Albany Medical Center Hospital and fussed her into the emergency room. She was four hours in labor, pain like she'd never even imagined, as her bones arduously stretched to respond to the imperative of birth. Sly paced and smoked and drank coffee, which frayed his nerves worse.

When the babe was far enough down the canal, Anika was given a spinal shot, an epidural, that numbed her from the waist down, and a vaginal cut, an episiotomy, so she wouldn't tear. The pain eased up so she could push more.

Sally arrived breathlessly during the labor, leaving the minute Sly called, wasting no time showering before rushing to Anika's birthing. She waved both hands in excited encouragement to her daughter, who smiled weakly. Anika blew her mom a kiss.

Sally, no particular fan of Sly's, stood with him watching through the glass as Anika panted through her pushing. "Andrew is so disappointed he has to work this morning of ALL mornings," she apologized. "Oh-my-GOSH it's happening!" She got big-eyed as she saw dark hair appear. She clutched at Sly's arm.

"I can't believe Anika doesn't even care that all these strangers are looking up her crotch!" She grimaced at Sly. "The queen of modesty herself."

"Yeah, hunh?" He nodded in shared amazement, never taking his eyes off Anika. "Doubt she cares at a time like this. She's too busy trying to breathe." He chuckled, licking his teeth.

"I'm sorry Andrew can't be here too," Sly murmured, aware that her family didn't care much for him. He knew Andrew judged him least as a former drinker himself. This was Sly's chance to redeem himself in this honored role of father of the first-born grandchild in Anika's clan.

"Oh LOOK! Do you believe this awesome wonder? Oh GOD," she whispered. Her hands went to her cheeks, her mouth open in a wondrous O.

Now, a full showing of dark hair. After a wait, a huge push from weary mom and out slid a little forehead. Then teeny closed eyes. And then, after another strained push, a nose, a tiny squinched-up face, cottage-cheesy, a little bloody. Their own amazing babe.

Sly said in amazement, "Lookit the strength of that woman! She's so *tough*," proudly, as Anika gave a strong push and baby's shoulders slid out, then a round little butt. Then the whole baby girl. "OH. MY. GOD!" He hugged Sally in irrepressible joy. They jumped up and down, lifted up by shared joy.

They watched the doctor hold her upside down and flick her little foot so she'd cry out the birth fluids. She let out an indignant bellow. Swiftly somebody put drops in her eyes. Sally said excitedly, "So that's her little voice! Get used to it, Dad."

The doctor reached in to ease the placenta out. Anika's heart burst open as a nurse placed her baby on her chest. Baby leaned on her forearms and looked in Anika's face for a moment, then dropped her tired little head on Anika's neck.

Anika glowed, grinning at Sly and her mom, then closed her eyes and breathed deep. She quickly opened them wide as if remembering the miracle anew. "Ain't she somethin'!" she murmured. "Ain't this just amazing!"

Bright morning sun streamed into the birthing room. The smell of freshly mown grass hung lightly in the air. Sally picked out from the surrounding sounds a Carolina wren singing its big-throated song in the tall sycamore outside the window. "All is right with the world—hallelujah," it trilled to her.

As the labor room staff worked their clean-up tasks, some smiling a little in the privilege of their work, the doctor paused to remove a glove, then stroked Anika's hair in a moment of grace.

"Good job, mum. You're a brave one, and that's one perfect baby. And did you see her lean up and check you out? Congratulations, and now get some rest." He rested his hand on her head a moment in a blessing. "Come show her off to us soon for your six-week checkup." He waved and mouthed "Congratulations" to Sally and Sly, flashing them a thumbs-up, and left.

After a carefully monitored rest, Anika was wheeled to her room, babe to the nursery. All vital signs were normal with both of them. This birth had gone well. Sly and Sally were waiting, drinking coffee from Styrofoam cups. Anika said sleepily, "We'll call her Cassie Anne, then, like we said? Wouldn't hurt to make Aunt Cassandra proud, combining our two names." She dropped her chin, smiling a little contented smile, and slept.

Sly nodded, touching her face tenderly. He had no words in that moment, just sat on the edge of her bed, stroking her hair. He leaned in to whisper, "You're the best, Annie. You're such a great mom already. I will have to hustle to be *half* the dad I wanta be for her," Anika nodded encouragement ever so slightly, reaching out to hold his hand through her weariness.

"Did you call your mom?" she murmured, eyes closed.

"Yeah. She was real happy. Said to tell you congratulations." Sly's dad had since died, and he didn't have much to say to his mother, who was now diabetic, an invalid.

Sally kept silence to honor the new family, grateful that mom and babe were healthy. She excused herself and went out to call Andrew.

"She's here, honey! And you know, the sun *does* rise and set in her, like you said," she laughed, sharing his prejudice about his two grandkids. "Annie was such a trooper. Amazing. Oh, they're naming her Cassie Anne, combo of Anika and Cassandra. Isn't that perfect?" Her voice was in high energy mode.

"Congratulations, you far-out grannie. Have I told you yet today that I love you?"

32

Peter—*A Year Later*

One fine spring morning in the shade of an oak tree, Anika came out with year-old Cassie Anne to watch her brother work on the bike. Peter thought Sly's cycle a typically selfish indulgence and helped out only for Anika's sake. He smiled tenderly at his little niece.

"Hi, Pee," Cassie Anne shouted and held out her arms to him. He threw her in the air. She squealed with joy, then lurched up and down to prompt him to keep it up.

"Hi, Pee!" Anika laughed, delighted to see him. His shirt was off in the heat. What a physique, she thought. But something was different—oh, his eyes were showing! Anika got it that Peter always wore sunglasses around Sly, hiding his hatred. Sly knew Pete despised him and flaunted his bully power worst in front of Peter. *Pissing contest, these male beasts,* she realized, shuddering.

Cassie Anne had struck a flame in Peter's heart, to his constant pleasure. He would look in on her as she slept and, when she woke, hold her tenderly to his chest. He loved the way she snuggled into him, the sweet smell of her, the little cooing sounds, all of it. He dreamed of having his own babes one day.

"Can I take her for a ride, sis?" he joked.

"Sure, we got some leathers and a helmet here somewhere." She laughed at the vision. "That girl has you wrapped around her little finger. You're so good with her."

He watched as Sly finished a beer. 10:00 a.m. Ignoring Anika and the baby, Anika trying to make everything work—a repeat of Carlos and Sally. Peter seethed and put on his sunglasses.

"Annie, get me another beer, hunh?" Sly said from his workbench. Not even a please.

"Already?" she said with an edge to her voice. She knew all too well where this day was going when the drinking started this early. "What about your promise to take Cassie Anne to the park?"

"And spare me the wisecracks, okay?" Sly shot back at her. "Whaddya think every other red-blooded vet is doing right about now in his own garage?"

So—we're gonna play the vet card again. The I-work-hard-to-support-this-family-so-back-off card, Peter saw. He shot a look of understanding to Anika, who shrugged as if to say, "Men. What can you do?"

A lifetime of watching abuse while he stood by helplessly, forced into silence by his father's violence. Now he was a man, a full-fledged protector of the women he loved.

The phone rang. Anika took Cassie Anne from Peter and went to answer it. It was Cassandra. Anika joked about the male noncommunication going on. "Fools!" she said laughing. "What prize do they think the winner gets, anyway?"

"You." Cassandra knew Anika didn't see her power in this triangle.

"Me? What do I possibly have that *they* want?" Cassandra was on to something here, but what?

"They both adore you, Annie."

"Oh my god, Cass. I never ever would have thought of that. Whoa. Let me chew on that for a minute. Keep talking."

"What this is really about is Sly's drinking and carousing, and watching that, Pete is seeing a rerun of Dad. Al-Anon calls it the elephant in the living room. 'Nobody admits there's a drunk in the house consuming everything decent, just tiptoes around it. Everybody gets crazy playing the shaky game, okay? Got your parts, everybody?'"

Cassandra was exercising the take-responsibility-for-oneself rights she was learning in Al-Anon. "My red-head privilege," she claimed, twisting the phone cord around her pointer finger. "Finally getting to the truth of what the *hell* was going on in our family and why I've felt so con*fus*ed in relationships. I'm *so* glad you and Allie are coming to Al-Anon. It's medicine. Right?"

"Wow, Cass. That's a lot to digest. You're good, Sis. I'll chew on that awhile. Amazing."

Out in the yard, Peter had an impulse. *Sly will want to test out the adjusted carburetor soon. If I loosen one of the brake couplings just enough that Sly won't detect it but a little normal vibration could jar it loose, it'll shake him up. I could feign forgetfulness if the son-of-a-bitch catches on, which is unlikely when he'll be thinking about the carburetor.*

Forgive me, Annie. This is how guys settle things. Scare the bejesus out of him. Peter left to shoot some hoops with Father Joe. "Don't ride this thing yet. Needs a part. I'll stop at the cycle shop. Back in a couple of hours," he mumbled to Sly.

He told Father Joe what he'd done. Father Joe stopped mid-dribble. "You did WHAT? No. You didn't. You idiot. That's called murder, Pete, for god's sake. What the *hell* are you thinkin'?"

Peter stopped still. "Right again, Father Joe. I'm going back there to fix it. Talk to you later." Peter left Father Joe praying in the middle of the court, went straight to Anika's, replaced the part, tightened the coupling, and slunk home without anyone seeing him.

Sly awoke with the hangover from hell Sunday. He vowed one more time to stop drinking. *And this time I mean it. A long sweet bike ride will take care of this.*

"Hey, hon, I'll just sneak out for a short ride and then we'll go to the park. I promise." Sly looked a bit green around the gills to Anika's practiced eye.

Anika stuck out her lips and shook her head, not wasting any useless words. She was wrestling some cereal into Cassie Anne. *Business as usual,* she thought. *Self-centered pain in the ass. What does he think will happen when he drinks like a fish like his father and mine?* "C'mon, sweet, we're taking dolly to the park." Cassie Anne sparkled with anticipation. Anika stuck her tongue out at Sly as she passed by.

Sly took the bike out to his favorite drive along the Hudson River, loving how smoothly it hummed along. He was thoroughly enjoying the wind on his skin, the power of the bike between his legs, the freedom of open air movement.

Beautiful day. Life is good and damn *this hangover.* He smiled a satisfied smirk.

He went over a bump in the pavement and felt something give. He looked to see if anything was amiss, saw nothing, then mentally noted to check it all over when he got home. *Good thing Pete is so good at this. He keeps this puppy humming smooth and sweet. I should be nicer to the little punk. Next time I will be. After all, he's family, shit-ass though he is.*

He rounded a curve and came up behind a semi-truck with a load of lumber moving slowly. He grabbed both brakes and stopped two feet away from death. *MA-an, that was close. I gotta quit drinkin'. This is it.*

33

Sly—June 1962

"What is it with you, Dawg? You think you're entitled to screw anything that walks? You think everybody in the plant doesn't *know*, asshole? I'm getting so tired of hearin' all the daily smut that flows around you! Now *my* boss is talkin'." Clint slammed his hand hard enough on his desk to make his coffee jump and spill some. "GodDAMN. First-class woman at home, and that doll baby—Jesus, you perverted fool." Clint glared at Sly.

Sly slumped down in his chair. *I'm so busted. He's got me. Nothin' I can say. Just see how bad it gets and figure what to do when he's had his say. Musta been the new girl, Sandy. The straw that broke the camel's back.*

"I hoped you'd outgrow this crap. I took a long shot and put some trust in you. She-itt. All the integrity of a rattlesnake. I struggled with lust too, Dawg, but I grew up." He leaned back in his chair to think. After a minute, he looked straight at Sly with fire enough to burn metropolitan Albany, Troy, and Schenectady.

"Here's the deal. Two days off without pay. You *ever* fuck around again and next time, it's a month. If you ain't learned by then, you're out the door with a tattoo that reads Incorrigible Fool."

Sly stood and fumbled with his keys, head down. "Sorry, sir, for what it's worth." He stumbled down the stairs and headed for the nearest men's room. He sat in a stall and took stock.

Man, *I am fucked. I won't be able to lie my way outa the pay cut with Anika, even if I could fake goin' to work the two days off. She's gonna hit the roof, struggling to pay the bills with* full *pay. If she ever dreamt the extent of my screwin' around, she'd walk—and make me pay. She's no fool. An' that brush with death with the lumber truck last weekend—sure looks like my number has come up.*

He rubbed his temples hard, squirming around on the seat. *And the worst of it for me is I lost Clint's respect and I prob'ly can't earn it back. That man has shown me a lot, and this is how I repay him? Jesus H. Christ, I've turned into my old man, the worst loser that ever drew breath, the one I swore I'd never be like. And I'm ex**act**ly like him. Crraa-ap what a loser. And the worst of this shit is it isn't even fun anymore, the chase and the screw.*

And a new thought—*maybe I should just quit and get it over with. Start new somewhere else where nobody knows me. But nobody pays like this place.*

Sly felt hot tears force their trail down his cheeks. *Man. If Anika's family finds out, that's it, I'm finished with all of 'em. I'm on real shaky ground as it is. So what if I come clean with Annie, or tell her just enough to get her on my side? Nah, she'll know I'm lyin'. She's known all along I was screwing around. Come t' think about it—why has she stayed with me this long, knowing full well I was cheating the whole time? What is that woman* made *of?*

"Sly Starner, please report to the power unit area," the loudspeaker broke in. "Sly Starner, power unit area."

Oh fuck. *I gotta go out there and face people, and this is prob'ly all over the plant by now. That's Sandy's work area—oh shit. What now?* He blew his nose on toilet paper and headed out to the floor. The few people he passed smirked at him. He glowered back at them. *Fuckin' people love to gloat when your ass falls off. Like they're any better? Yeah right.*

He approached the power unit area and saw Sandy over by the parts shelf, away from her team. She jerked her head to signal him over. "I'm done, Sly. Don't come around no more." She turned on her heel and picked up a wrench to torque a bolt on the unit she was building. She stuck her chin up high and proud.

Sly turned and left. *Well, that's it. Everything I've touched has turned to shit. I wonder if I can even salvage my marriage now. Will Anika even let me see Cassie Anne?*

"Sly Starner, report to the tool crib. Sly Starner, tool crib, please," barked the loudspeaker.

He had a buddy in the tool crib. *Maybe a breath of air here*, he dared to hope. He met some eyes on his walk down the long aisle. Most just looked away. One wise guy gave him an evil grin, and he had all he could do not to flatten him. *Weaslin' punk!*

At the tool crib, his pal, Jimmy, motioned him over. Sly knew Jimmy likely knew what was up. He'd been here so long and had an ear to the ground. Jimmy was a square-built guy, around fifty, lead man in his area, straight-talking and fair. Hardly anyone could touch him when he had a cue stick in his hand.

"Heard it caught up t' ya, Dog, ya dumb shit. 'Bout time with yer reckless whorin'. Any diseases shrivel that thang up yet?"

"Nah, Jimmy. Deep dumb shit fer sure. No diseases, I'm pretty careful. Clint gi' me two days. Anika's gonna bust a gut. An' I nearly bought the farm on the bike the other day. Come up behind a big ol' lumber truck fast and about wiped out. Tied one on the night before." Sly took off his safety glasses and wiped his tear-burned eyes. "Gotta clean up my act, Jim. Ain't much more to lose. How'd you do it? You tell some wild stories . . . what reined you in, bud?"

"I lost my fam'ly 'fore I sobered up. Did some time in the lockup. Damn lucky my kids even talk t' me. One day I just had enough. Hung up my spurs an' parked my ass in AA. Been savin' a seat fer you there, looney tune. You finally ready or d'ya need to lose some more?"

"Ah, I dunno, Jim. I ain't a drunk like my old man. I just ferget t' quit some nights." Sly scraped a spot on the floor with his steel-toed boot.

"Yeah right. How many nights you 'tip a few' as you call it? An' don't bullshit a bullshitter." Jimmy looked over the rim of his glasses, steely-eyed.

"Uh, maybe three, four. Nah that's a damn lie. Pretty much ever' night, Jim. Yeah, I'd have t' say every night. Anika's given up, guess because her dad did it too." He thought awhile. "Ya know, Jim, I'll bet it's killin' her. Amazing woman loves me, but she hates what I do."

Jimmy let him talk, knowing what guts it took to confess this monkey on his back—more like a gorilla. He genuinely wanted to help Sly. And he knew how, and when. He sponsored a few guys in AA. He knew AA's best gift to new candidates was listening, letting them hear themselves think it through, especially at this humbling time when their lives were crumbling in a heap on the floor. Sly was ready for help.

"Think about it, Dawg. This only gets worse if you don't face up to it fair and square. You got a dose of the disease and it wants you dead." Jimmy touched his shoulder kindly.

"Thanks, Jim. I will." Sly left to lick his wounds and think. He dreaded what was to come with Anika.

34

Anika—June 1962

Anika heard Sly's slow footsteps on the walkway at his usual arrival time. *Now what?* she thought. She stirred the chicken she was frying, looking at Cassie Anne playing on the floor with pots and lids, and said, "Daddy's home, sweety."

Cassie looked up brightly, squealing "Dada? Dada!" as he rounded the doorway. He got down on his knees to hold his little girl close.

Somethin's up, Anika's heart told her. "So how was your day, Dawg?" She stirred the beans and the rice pilaf, waiting.

"You are about as cute as a button, little girl. Did you and Mommy have fun today?" His voice sounded choked.

Anika leaned over to look in his face, wiping her hands on her apron. Wo. Dark place. "What happened?" She stroked his face and lifted his chin in her hand, looking close in to read his face.

"Annie. Do you love me?" He struggled to his feet, holding Cassie Anne.

Anika lowered her eyes. *Now there's a loaded question. Let me sort through my ten thousand feelings.* She looked straight in his eyes, taking a big breath. "At times I do, when you're here and kind. When you drink and sleep around, no. I hate you then." *This is the part where Dad would slap Mom. Would Sly? While he's holding Cass even?*

Sly put Cass down carefully, then stood to reach for Anika. He held her in a bear hug for a long moment. Cassie Anne wedged between their legs. "Mama Dada?" She was laughing up into their faces.

Sly's belly spasmed. Anika felt it. He spoke through the sea urchin lodged in his throat.

"Look, Annie, I screwed up at work and got two days off. I'm gonna cut some firewood with Jimmy to make up the money. And it's not important what happened at work, so please let's leave that alone. Here's what is important, hon." He held her at arm's length. Shame closed his eyes as he said, "I had a wake-up last weekend I didn't wanta tell you about and scare you. I nearly wiped out on the bike when I was hung over. Annie, I'm done. I'm done drinkin' and hangin' in bars and tryin' t' be my old man. I'm done, baby."

Cassie echoed "I done, ba-by!"

Anika burst out laughing, reached to hug her, saying, "Daddy's come home, baby. Daddy's goo-od." She kissed Cass and then Sly.

"Well, okay then. What help are you gonna need?"

"God, you're amazing, woman. You're about the strongest person I've ever met. Damn I've got a lot to learn from you." He felt a tear push through and down his cheek. That's when she saw he meant it.

"Sly. I've gone to Al-Anon, and I'm really hopeful about the power of that program to help me heal from all the crap of alcoholism. Mom's going, and Cass, now Allie even. I wonder if AA could help you get sober. This would be the perfect time to check it out."

"Yeah, that's what Jimmy said. Think I'll give it a try. What've I got to lose?"

"Sly, this is amazing. This could make all the hell we've both been through worth the journey. Let's do this, baby."

"You must have been God-sent to be my own particular angel. I love you, Annie, big time. I swear I'll make this all up to you. You are so worth it. And this little girl . . ."

"Pigtime," the little echo sang out. Sly held her in front of him to look in her eyes. "You, my doll baby, are the best of all the rest."

"I bes'!" She hugged her daddy in a neck-bender squeeze. She nodded at her mama over his shoulder. "Yup. I bes'."

35

Peter—September 1962

Peter now lived in the apartment Sally and Andrew built for him over their garage, a cozy spot fashioned in log cabin style, rustic and comfortable with a skylight over his bed. Picking slowly through college, studying literature and working at a motorcycle shop, he was steadily gaining a reputation for fine machine maintenance. Thus he had the means to branch out into his first love of writing and reading.

Pete got interested in the Students for a Democratic Society movement when a friend took him to a rally led by the dynamic Stokely Carmichael. He caught the pulse of the rising drumbeat of the '60s and felt a quickening in his soul, the spark he'd been waiting for all through his early years. This was his time to come alive with ideas that were catching on all over the country.

Driving home from class one night with Anika, he turned to her and burst out,

"Annie, I've never known the stars to line up like this before! These guys are saying the Vietnam War is bullshit, that peace is the only long-term way to solve conflicts. Well *yeah*. Did you see the Vietnamese monk immolate himself on the news last night? And women and black folks deserving equal rights? This is the prevailing wind I've waited for all along—freedom and justice for all—what a concept. Guys dodging the draft for moral reasons. Whada*you* think of it all?"

"I'm so in too, Pete. It's like the country is waking up to what us kids knew was crazy all along, and now we have a collective voice. Really exciting times. Makes me scared for Cassie Anne though—what kind of a world is she gonna inherit? Guess that calls me to action, hunh? To create the change

---

I believe in, like Nelson Mandela says—I *think* it was him—to *be* the change we believe in?" She drove along in silence.

"So where does this lead you, bud?" she wanted to know.

"Makes me want to write and teach writing all the more. I think that's my niche, sis, to wake up kids' minds to big thinkers like Black Elk, Martin Luther King Jr., Abraham Lincoln, Bobby Kennedy. To challenge kids to risk thinking out of the box with their own ideas. Shake it up, get creative. Make education come alive." Peter tapped his cigarette ash out the window. "School doesn't have to be the boring drudge it's been forever. So, babe, how're you and Sly doin', and my little buddy-pal?"

"Well, bro, that little monkey is riding her tricycle all the way to the park and back now. No stopping her. Thinks she's got the world by the seat of the pants, so I guess she does. Lots more words now, some of them even understandable. And she talks to everybody—all strangers are fair game for her irrepressible babble. It's fun going places with her and watching her charm the pants off people." She glanced at him to share a chuckle about the sweetness of the child they both adored.

"And her da—you're not gonna believe this. Gimme a drumroll. The Sly Dawg is sobering up. Stop the world, hunh? He went to an AA meeting with a buddy from work, and he came home all happy and smiling. Sly, happy. When donkeys fly, hunh? The earth moved. He plays with Cassie, he comes home from work on time. He helps around the house. I can hardly believe it—surely, aliens have stolen my sorry-assed husband. He's *nice*, you believe that? I only pray it lasts."

"Whaddya think caused it—I mean the sudden sobriety attack?" Peter said, surprised.

"Well, when you fixed his bike, what, a couple of months back? He took it out for a spin the next morning. He had tied a good one on night before so he was lookin' green around the gills, pretty foggy. He says he came around a turn and all but slammed into a big lumber truck crawling along with a heavy load. That got his attention. And then he got time off from work for some kind of screw up he doesn't wanna talk about. Probably a woman. None of my business, I'm learning in Al-Anon, so I don't snoop. It all came together in the right time to make him look for a new perspective. And AA seems to be giving him just that. Amazing, hunh? If that ain't God showing off, you tell me what is! I'm holding my breath in case it doesn't last. But it's been a couple of months now, and he's still going to AA and looking like a newbie on the planet. AMAZing."

"Annie baby, I'm just gonna say this one time cuz I know you'll shoot me down like you always do. But—this is the effect you have on people. You are a born counselor, the energizer Gumby. You give people the shot in the arm we need to get up and fight the good fight. And you do it without judgment, without pretense, just natural-like, which is why it works. So who better to get the benefit of your good spirit than your old man? I swear you and Mom—you're made of supernatural stuff."

Anika stared at the road and blinked.

"REALly, bro. I felt that somewhere deep, Pete. And it feels true so I gotta receive it and let it grow in me, right?"

"Bingo, sis. Thanks for hearing me and not just blowing it off. You've got the goods, pal. And the desire to use your gift. Now just get that degree and go use it for God's purposes."

"Aw shucks, Pete. That's huge. Especially coming from my favorite brother."

36

Family Time—November 1962

Sally and Andrew kept Zack's kids while Zack and Cassandra planned a gala weekend away in celebration of his divorce. Sally took pains to make meals kids would like—pizza and mac and cheese and pancakes with their initials imprinted on top. And big bowls of homemade French vanilla ice cream which they took turns hand-cranking.

Peter came over for breakfast Saturday morning and afterward shot hoops with them. Andrew lobbed a few mostly from the sidelines, complaining good-naturedly all the while about arthritic knees and getting old as just desserts for wimps and drunks. He did manage to take them hiking in Thatcher Park in the afternoon, using a branch he broke off for support, or leaning heavily on the kids when they got too close. They loved his antics. "You're getting mean in your old age, Gramps," Kiera whimpered.

Sunday morning. They piled into Andrew's old Volkswagen van, his granddad wagon, and rattled off to Father Joe's church where he was now senior priest. They picked up Marymoll on the way. "Y'er too kind t' me, ye are, an' that's the truth," she grinned.

"You're family, old dear, so you hafta go where this cranky old van goes, and try to get along," Andrew teased her. He only picked on those he found worthy.

"Not that I ever wanted to be anything but a kid's priest, playin' more basketball than preachin'," Father Joe told them after the service. "But ya go where the Boss tells ya, like it or not." He jerked his thumb upward as he said Boss. "And they're good to me, don't fall asleep *every* time I'm talkin'." He grabbed Marymoll with a hearty bear hug. "How's my own girl? Man, it's been too long. You are one Irishwoman I dearly miss." He held her out to have a look at her. She grinned at the familiar crinkle of his eyes.

"It's because ye rub the Blarney stone s' good b'farr ye step up t' th' podium, me man. Sure 'n' it's *good* t' see ya." She held his face in a blessing moment.

Peter waited while he was introduced to the kids and chatted up with Andrew and Sally. "Hey, old coot. Been too long. You're lookin' wonderful," he said, as he hugged Father Joe long and well. "Man, I miss you."

"You look great, bud. Handsome as you wanta be. And grown into a man for real. Any chance you have time for a catch-up chat in my office?"

"Sure, I'll just tell Mom we'll be a minute." Peter gave Sally a heads-up so they could go feed the kids and come back for him.

"So, Pete. What's been happenin'?" the priest asked, as they settled in his comfortable office.

Peter just wanted to bask in his presence. "Man, this is sweet, like old times. You look as good as ever. Still playin' hoops?"

"Not as much without you to smack me around out there. But when I can. So tell me. What're you up to?"

"Livin' at Mom's in the apartment they built me over the garage. Nice. Still chippin' away at that degree and working on cycles now, trying to teach bikers how to maintain their machines. I think a lot about the Vietnam War and where this country is headed. This is a good time to be coming up, know what I mean? Pretty alive times—lots of changes."

"Pete. You do my heart good, sounding so clear and inquisitive. So where's all this taking you?"

"Teaching, writing, looks like. It's what gets me up in the mornin', so I guess it's my path. Next semester, I start student teaching, so that's when I'll know more. I wrote some poetry I like and am trying to get it published." Peter cleared his throat.

Father Joe leaned back, hands folded behind his head "You are following your heart well, bud. I'm real proud of you. Real proud." He rubbed his palms together. "So how's my friend, Anika, and Sly? And Allie?"

"You'll like this—Sly is sober in AA, making some good changes. Remember that day I messed with his brakes on his cycle and came and told you, and you chewed my butt bad? He nearly wiped out next day, then some trouble at work, and he woke up. Anika's so much happier, he's even a dad now. She's still in school too, working toward a counseling degree, scraping by on loans like me. That Cassie Anne is a hoot—you'd love her. Got a lot of spunk." Pete looked over at Father Joe's bookshelves intently. He glanced at Father Joe in a shy way.

"Allie? She's good, teaching middle school, still real close with Annie. I'm trying to work up the courage to ask her out. Whaddya think, too incestuous? Zack and Cassandra, me and Allie?"

"Nah, it's just who you like. She's a terrific girl, always has been. We talk about spiritual stuff still and it's real lively for me. Sharp woman. Go for it, why not? Bet she's waiting for you to ask."

"All right, I will. You've never steered me wrong yet. Guess I better let you get on with your day, hunh? Thanks for the time. You're still the best, man."

"Don't be a stranger, my man. I love ya', Pete. Always have and always will." They held one another in a long sweet hug, and went on their way.

37

Sobriety—1962

Marymoll sat musing in her prayer time before dawn one drizzly Monday morning. She knew this was Anika's favorite time for sitting with God too, so she felt blessed twice in the sharing of the wonder with her young friend. She thanked God for the gift of Anika, so like a dear daughter to her. One prayer led to the next. She gave thanks for Father Joe's wisdom in guiding Peter along a good path, he who had seemed so lost in anger for much of his young life. She had often prayed for him as Sally had shared his struggles, and now she was seeing him progress along a good road.

She startled when her phone rang. She reached for it expectantly, knowing it could only be Anika at this hour. "Good marnin' dearest," she said brightly. "Jes' thinkin' o' ye."

Anika laughed gladly. "And what if it were the mayor's office calling you and you answered like that? But not at 6:00 a.m., you're right again." She remembered why she'd called. "Oh, it's good to hear your voice, to be able to call *you* in these precious quiet hours. Got some good news for you, some results of all that amazing praying you do. Guess who is getting sober?"

"Oh. M' GAWD! Oh, baby—oh dear Gawd. How'd he do it?"

"Couple of factors. Near wreck on the motorcycle when he was hung over, and trouble at work that got him a time out. But the important thing is, it's God working things out, don't you think? The timing *and* the combination of the two events *and* his own readiness? A bit more than coincidental? Anyway, I'm blown away. I got my husband back, and Cass has a real daddy. He's even going to AA, Marymoll, can you believe that? And he likes it. Says it's helping him figure his head out."

"Well, don't that beat all," Marymoll marveled. "'Mebbe all them prayers I've been wearin' His ears out with are workin' after all."

"Bless your heart, you always know and support what I'm feeling. You're the best person to talk to when the wolf is at the door. Thank you so much for being in my life, old dear. Such a great listening ear."

"Well, ye gi' me a lotta strength, just by bein' s' strong an' good-hearted. Ye've grown up straight and fine like yer good mama. I sure am grateful fer ye—I was just tellin' m' Friend. I could feel Him smilin'. He likes ye too." She laughed. "How's m' little one doin'?"

"She's kinda off her feed, Marymoll. Teething, maybe. Cranky and snuffly. Just when I have a tough paper to write."

"Why not bring her over t' me t' watch while ye write? I'd luv t' play with 'er t'day. It'd keep me off the streets."

"You're a riot. You sure you want the little bean? I don't want her to give you a cold or something."

"Bring 'er by. I'll bake some chocolate chips wi' 'er and send some home t' ye fer comfort food while ye write yer paper, an' fer congratulashuns t' Sly. How's that? Oh, I'm near out a' brown sugar, you got any?"

"Sure, hon, I'll bring it. Around ten-ish then? And, Marymoll, thanks for your prayers for Sly and for me. Darned if they don't do the trick."

They said goodbye and went for the last of their coffee pots and their contemplation hour.

Sly came drowsily downstairs to her then, softly to not wake Cassie Anne. He snuggled close to her on the couch. "Have I told you yet today how much I love you?" he whispered in her ear.

She wriggled close to him. "Sly? It's you and not a ghost clone the aliens replaced my husband with to tease me and then snatch him away and put the old creep back in place?"

He wrapped his arms around her and sat a long moment in perfect contentment. "Remind me what the hell I was thinkin' back there--no, don't. God this is sweet. sweet, my beautiful Anika."

38

Peter and Allie

Just before dawn, Peter got up to finish a world history paper before work on a clear cold morning. He yawned, took a sip of strong coffee, and dove in.

He was attempting to compare the Vietnam War to the Christian crusades, demonstrating the futility of war as solution to any complex international or ideological issue. He cited President John F. Kennedy's action in the Cuban missile crisis as a prime example of conflict resolution by negotiation. He had come to admire Kennedy as a leader with the heart and courage to think globally and act specifically, effectively.

His research had shown him just how complex the conflicting interests facing Kennedy and the United Nations—how politically and economically expedient war was for some power factions, and how "soft" Kennedy opponents could portray him to be on the world stage, particularly up against Khrushchev and the powerful Soviet Union. A misstep in perception could be hazardous to the US's role as stabilizer of world peace, to say nothing of Kennedy's political career. Peter was learning tons and shaping his mind as potential educator, excited to be forming his own worldviews.

He typed the last of the bibliography as his phone rang. *It must be Anika at this pre-dawn hour.* She was the only soul he knew who liked rising at this quiet time of the day.

But it wasn't. It was Allie.

"Pete, were you up at this insane hour?" she apologized.

"Sure, Al, but I thought you must be Annie at this crazy time. I've been working on a paper that's due tonight. But hey—nobody in the world makes

---

phone calls at 6:00 a.m. so I'm guessing this is important? Not that it has to be . . ." Peter had to shower and make lunch for work shortly.

"Well, um, Pete, Annie said you were hip to the SDS and that you went to a Stokely Carmichael rally?" She was beginning to regret calling at this hour or wondering if she should have called at all. "Could we get together and talk about it sometime? I'm reading up on the SDS stuff and I'd like to pick your brain. If you want . . . I know you're real busy with school and all," she said shyly.

"Yeah, Allie, I'd be real glad to have that talk with you. Are you free Friday night? Maybe we could get a beer somewhere."

"Sounds great. How's Mike's Log Cabin? Pick me up around eight?"

"You bet, Al. Your place at eight. Somethin' to look forward to while I torque bike bolts all day. See you then. And, Allie—thanks for callin'. You beat me to it."

~~~

Friday night finally came around. Pete was prompt. "Hi, Aunty." He smiled, genuinely glad to see Allie's friendly aunt who most people just called Aunty. "How're things with you?" he asked, as he stepped inside.

"Peter! How great to see you. Handsome as ever. How's school? And how's your mama?" She led him into her favorite room for close conversation—her kitchen. "Glass of something? Water? Iced tea?"

"Maybe some water, thanks. Mom's great, likes being married to Andrew a whole lot. School's good, keeps me on my toes after playing grease monkey all day. How's Tom?" Peter was never much for small talk.

Aunty brought his water and sat with him. "Oh, you know, grumpy old fart that he is. Not happy if he's not complaining about somethin' or other."

Allie came in then, looking perky and, Peter thought, stunning. He blushed crimson and stood to greet her, not knowing what to do with his hands, so he fumbled them behind his back.

"Hey, Allie-girl. You look great. You surviving those junior high brats?"

"Somehow, some days, Pete." She laughed. "Aunty, you gonna be all right alone? Uncle Tom playing poker like usual on Fridays?"

"Thanks, honey, but you kids run along. I love my Friday nights to myself." She kissed Allie's cheek and gave Peter a warm hug. *Love you, dear kids*, she whispered to their departing backs.

Peter and Allie were on their way.

39

Anika

Anika awoke at 3:00 a.m. Quiet. No breathing next to her. She reached over to Sly's side of the bed. No one.

She screamed into her pillow. "SHIT. I knew it couldn't last!" She thrashed around the bed raging, crying, and planning her escape. After a while she grew quiet, frozen in confusion. *What to do now?* She tried praying but couldn't concentrate.

She heard a soft sound on the stairs. *Prowler? Probably not.* Sly slipped quietly in the room, into the bed. She rolled over toward him, sniffing. Coffee and cigarettes.

"I know why you're thinking what you're thinking, baby. But I didn't drink. Prob'ly a good thing there's no booze here." He shifted onto his side, facing her. "I couldn't sleep and didn't want to wake you so I went downstairs to read some AA stuff and make coffee. Then I heard you yelling into your pillow so I came to check on you. I get why you're freakin' out, babe. No wonder. I love you, babe, and I'm tryin' harder than I've ever tried for anything. I'm gonna beat this, Annie, before it kills me and us and Cass." He choked up.

Anika lay on her back looking at the ceiling, hands cradling her head. "Sorry, hon. I reacted out of old stuff. I'm still gun-shy. I know you're tryin' hard now, but old crap creeps into my head when I wake and you're not here, after all those nights of wondering where you were. And all those nights of listening to Mom worry about where Dad was. I'm trying to live in the present like Al-Anon is teaching me but I'm scared of getting blindsided again. I want to trust but . . . I want to stay awake too."

She rolled over to him. "There's something else, Sly. Since I started Al-Anon and praying and meditating, I've been waking around 3:00 a.m. many mornings. When you're here I just lie still so I don't disturb you and eventually go back to sleep. But it's getting old. It's getting to be every night."

"Don't know about that, baby. Have you talked with Miz Marymoll? She's usually good for you to ask about stuff like that."

"Good idea. I'll talk to her. Maybe I'll call Father Joe. G'night. And Sly—good work, hon. I'm real proud of you. *Thank* you. I truly love you."

She read an article in an acupuncture magazine claiming that the hours between 3:00 a.m. and 5:00 a.m. were the prime hours of spiritual development on the Chinese clock.

"Makes sense," she told Allie on the phone the next time they talked. "It's when we're still and the world is silent—no distractions, so God can get our attention. It's like an alarm goes off, my eyes pop open, and it's right about three or a little after, every time."

"I've heard of that. I read a book about the diary of a mystic whose night visions always happened about that time, 3:00 a.m. Funny how these things that seem so unique turn out to be commonplace. Universal even, sometimes." Allie shifted the receiver to her other ear. "So what are you getting from it? It seems like a real gift, like an appointment with the Holy One."

Anika sipped her coffee. "I've tried to fight it and go back to sleep, but forget that. Now I just say, 'Okay. What's up?' It *is* amazing. I get this feeling of being held, cared about, even cherished, dare I say it? And I get guidance about all kinds of stuff."

"That makes sense during this time of change with Sly, Annie. How's he doing, by the way?"

"You're gonna laugh. I woke at three the other morning and felt for him, and he was gone. I *lost* it. Started screaming *asshole* into my pillow and crying and figuring out how to get a divorce. And then he slipped into bed, smelling of coffee and smokes."

"Wow, babe. What did you say?"

"I apologized for reacting out of fear, and he understood, and we went on." Anika breathed deeply. "He is trying so hard, Al. I give him a whole lot of A for effort. He's reading AA literature, going to meetings, and not picking up that first drink, all the stuff he's supposed to do. He even talks to his friend at work like a sponsor and lets the guy kick his butt. But I keep waiting for him to screw up. What *is* my *problem*?"

"History is your problem, Goof. Give it time, and pray, right? Isn't that what Reds told you? How could you unlearn a lifetime of betrayal by alcoholics overnight? Be gentle with yourself. God is working this out and

His plans are a little bigger than you can see. Hey—you think that's Him waking you up at three while you're a captive audience? What if you just listen for that still small voice? Maybe that's God showing Himself out in the open, which He doesn't do half enough, if I have anything to say about it."

"Al, uhm . . . something interesting came out of my time with Him the other night. You ready for this?" She pulled an afghan around her legs.

"It must be big, with *this* build-up. And about me. Lay it on me." Allie crossed her arms, cradling the receiver against her shoulder.

"Allie, I saw you and Peter together. There. I said it."

"Wha-at? What did you actually see? I mean, what were we doing?" Allie felt a flush all through her face and neck.

"You were running with your backs to me. And you were looking at each other, smiling, clearly a couple, like it was good between you."

"Whoa. And you say God gave you this vision? Not that it hasn't crossed my mind . . ." Allie cleared her throat. "So okay, I guess I forgot this important part. We went out for a beer and a talk about SDS and politics and stuff the other night. I called him to ask if we could talk, and he asked me out, and we had a really good talk. Don't know if we'll go out again, but it was nice, Annie."

"Let me get this straight," Anika said slowly. "You went out with *my* brother who never dates for a date and didn't tell me. Right, best friend. I get it. This wasn't important enough to pick up the phone." Anika was only half joking.

"*I* know—chicken, I guess. I guess I like him a whole lot more than I've admitted, Annie. Sorry."

"And I guess you think I haven't noticed all these years. Right. Now who's the goof? Oops . . . better go—sounds like the munchkin is up."

"I'll come by later and take Cassie Anne out for a walk, okay?"

"Great, thanks. And—Al—I'm in, babe. I'd love you and Pete together."

"Well okay then. Later, 'gator."

40

Allie—1963

Teaching was so natural to Allie that she felt almost guilty taking a paycheck. She told her aunty that if the district coffers ran dry, she'd find a way to teach under a tree for free, it was that important to her. "These kids' minds are sponges, given decent presentation. Their eyes light up and they start sparking, and I feel like I've handed them the moon. But in fact, they've handed *me* the sun. The administration—now that's a whole 'nother can of worms. They show me how much I *am* earning my keep."

"Nice. You're earning back all the hours of bitching I've endured from Tom, paying for your education." She thumped her breast in mock martyrdom and snorted with laughter. Allie cracked up with her.

"So?" Aunty raised her eyebrows. "You gonna tell me about your date or am I gonna have to beat it out of you? You've been whistling a merry tune around here ever since Friday. IF someone were noticing." She cackled again.

"Well, Aunty dear. *IF* anyone were noticing, I gotta admit I'm smitten. Don't know what *he's* feeling because he didn't say. Gave me a little peck on the cheek as he dropped me off, just. But we talk really well together. I think we always have, actually. He's lighter than he used to be, happier. Come into his own, I guess. Smart! And *so* easy on the eyes. Yumm. I think we could go far together, Aunty."

"Well, there you have it, my girl. I hear the call of destiny." She cupped her ear, listening for distant drums, then shifted in her chair and looked at her nails over the rims of her glasses. "I've always liked Peter. I'm so glad he's working his way out of the shadows. That's courage, right there. How's my dear Sally?"

"Oh, she's real good. She and Andrew are so perfect together, so grateful for love to enjoy after the hard years. And you know, Zack and Cassandra have hooked up and that's a good thing. If Peter and I would get together, can you imagine the ring of fire? Thanks to Al-Anon and AA. Oh, I told you, right? Sly is in AA now, hasn't drank for, I don't know, two months now? Annie is in shock. Cassie Anne is a different child—happy, huggy, sweet. Amazing." Allie wrapped her arms around her tummy and rocked back and forth, laughing at her happiness.

"Think I'm crazy to hope Pete and I get together?" she asked sincerely.

The phone rang. Allie went to answer it. "Oh hi, Pete. Aunty and I were just talkin' about, uhm, your mom and them." She raised her eyebrows up and down at Aunty and scooted around the corner for privacy.

"So, Al. How're things with you?" His voice sounded a little choked. *He's scared*, she thought. *Maybe he's feeling the same thing I am. Could it be? Oh God, don't let me screw this up **please**.*

"Good, Pete, how about you? Oh, I wanted to thank you for a really good talk the other night. I really enjoyed that."

"Well good then. Me too. Wondered if you'd like to take in a foreign film at school this weekend. There's a Jean-Paul Belmondo flick I've been wanting to see. Might Friday at eight work? I think it's only playing Friday, and then it changes. But it's your call."

"No, Friday's good. Pick me up around seven thirty then?"

"Cool. And, Allie, I like talking with you. You're easy to talk with."

There's that choked-up tone again. "Well, good, I'm glad, Pete. Me too. See you Friday then?"

She hung up and squealed into the kitchen. Aunty stood to hug her. "Couldn't happen to two nicer kids. What're you gonna wear?"

41

Tragedy—November 22, 1963

Peter was at work with the radio on WGY news. He had just finished the tuna sandwich he'd made for lunch and was biting into a firm McIntosh apple, sitting on his work stool, looking out at the sunny November afternoon. He was thinking about Allie and how good they were together, like he was discovering the great mystery of love that had eluded him until now, strangely familiar yet soul-expanding. His fear was slowly lessening as intrigue took its place.

"The president has been shot." Slower now. "President John F. Kennedy has been *shot.*" The announcer sounded incredulous.

Peter looked around the shop for some confirmation, shaking his head in shock. *What! What did he say? No, that's not possible.* He wiped his hands on his shop rag, trying to take this in.

"A Secret Serviceman has been wounded. First Lady Jacqueline Kennedy was unharmed, though bloody from trying to shield her husband. It is now official. The president is dead. Repeat. President John Fitzgerald Kennedy is dead."

Peter looked around the shop and caught the eye of the foreman, Jake, a wise aging hippie with a scruffy gray beard down to his chest. Peter was glad for an ally in this.

"Holy *shit,*" Jake hollered. "Did you *hear* that?" Jake's eyes bulged as he wiped his hands on his shop rag. "Tell me this is *not* happenin', Pete. Jesus H. Christ."

Peter's head dropped down on his chest. *Mother of* God. *Be with us all. Especially Kennedy's wife and family. What a hideous rotten turn of events.* Peter felt hot tears in his eyes and rubbed them. *Go with God, Mr. President.*

Peter realized that what he was doing was praying. *There's a first.*

After a while, he looked up at Jake, who was watching him, hands spread at his hips in disbelief. "Damn, Jake. DA-amn. The shit is gonna hit the fan, hunh? International chaos. Just when he seemed to have some forward momentum as world leader. I have a terrible feeling that this is the end of decency. Killing our own best from within—what message are we telling the world?" Peter held his fist to his forehead.

Jake came over and gave Pete an uncommon side hug, arm tight around his shoulders, and held it there. "Yeah, buddy, this is real big. Terrible. And so-o *stu*pid. Probably the Russians." Jake shook his head. "C'mon. Let's get outa here and grab a coffee, watch the news. I'm buyin'."

They walked down the street toward the coffee shop as though sleepwalking, shaking their heads again and again. Peter felt light-headed, foggy.

Jake said sadly, "Jesus. Do you believe this shit? Where's my acid when I need it?" He chortled, remembering the forty miles of bad road LSD had taken him down. They reached the restaurant and went in, looking around at the dazed faces glued to the TV, seating themselves close to it. Pete held two fingers up in request to the waitress who nodded, looking stricken, teary-eyed, mascara running down her cheeks.

There were murmurs of incredulous fear, shouts of disbelief, and angry threats from the stunned little crowd. On the TV, film clips tumbled through the events in Dallas, shocking the world with the terrible truth that the first world's leader could be brought down by a bullet in the light of an ordinary day. What was safe if this unthinkable thing could happen? A new and hideous notion was hitting the world's consciousness: this was an ugly new day. The world's compass was turning a few degrees south.

Peter said quietly in Jake's ear, "Is it too strong to say this is the end of innocence on the world stage, Jake? A high degree of evil?"

"I'm afraid you're right, son. Well put," Jake grumbled miserably. "God save us all." Jake tipped his cup toward Peter in a grim toast to what was to come.

They finished their coffees and headed back. Allie called Peter during her break that afternoon. "Pete. You okay?"

"Yeah, baby. You?"

"I'm stunned. Stupefied. The kids are all whacked out scared. This rocks their world big time. They called us all down to the auditorium for an assembly. The principal talked, pretty well for a change, thoughtful, concerned for the kids. Big blowup of Kennedy behind him. Then the guidance counselor said a few words, let the kids ask questions or make comments, and then we all gathered in a big closed circle, holding hands in silent vigil for a couple of minutes. It was well handled. Lot of sniffling."

"Nice work. Give the kids some substance to chew on. Set the tone for their thinking and doing it in community. How are *you* doin', babe?"

"I'd love to be with you for comfort tonight, Pete. Can I come over after work?"

"Sure. I need to be with you too. I'll whip us up some dinner, and we can watch it together."

"Love you, Pete."

"See you tonight. Love you too."

42

Transcendence

Sally cooked the Thanksgiving dinner for the whole clan, including booming Father Joe who was seated at the place of honor beside Andrew. Next to Sally at the foot of the table was smiley Miz Marymoll, hair softly turning white. Anika was beside her, looking bleary-eyed for lack of mommy sleep. Cassie Anne was getting over croup she'd caught at playgroup. Sly flanked her high chair, grateful to feel included in a warmer way now in his recovery. Peter was on Marymoll's other side, then Allie.

Cassandra was beside Zack's daughter, Keira, then his son, Tim, alongside his dad, all according to place cards. Cass sparkled, flashing glances at Zack, who looked entirely content.

Andrew tapped his water glass with his knife and stood to say the blessing. Zack took his neighbors' hands, and everyone followed. "Heavenly Father, I'm just standing in for Father Joe here, so please forgive my humble efforts while he rests for a change." He cleared his throat. Soft chuckles sounded around the table.

"Maker of all good things, we gather today to say a great big thank You for each one gathered here today. We are *so* richly blessed to have such a fine clan. Don't know what we've done to deserve any of it, Father, but thank You for every one of these your beloved children, and thank You that we all share one another's lives." Marymoll murmured a soft "Amen."

Andrew paused to catch up with his thoughts.

"Now comes the *please bless* part, Father, but You knew that, coming from me." Now everybody chuckled louder. Anika squeezed Marymoll's hand gently. Zack's kids sneaked smiling looks at each other sideways. Cassie Anne picked up the laughter and looks and squealed a high-pitched laugh, which broke everyone up. Her mother put a finger in front of her lips, and Cassie quieted down. Sly noted the child's listening of her mother and smiled in his heart.

Andrew continued his prayer. "Please bless the Kennedy family in this hideously difficult, so undeserved time of pain and loss, and let their hearts receive Your love through the fervent prayers of the entire known world. Please help the world stay calm through the storm, and teach us wisdom in our suffering. We know one thing—that You have our best interests at heart. For that, we give You high praise and grateful hearts. And"—he raised his water glass in toast to Sly—"here's to the miracle of sobriety. Amen." Andrew wiped his eyes and sat down. Amens sounded around the table. Sally raised her glass to her husband with a cocked head and glad smile.

Zack spoke next. "Thought you were gonna deliver one of those long-winded soliloquies of yours while Sally's wonderful food got cold." He smiled warmly at his dad. "Beautiful, Dad, thanks."

Cassandra beamed at him, then at Kiera, who dropped her eyes. Tim looked at his plate with mouth-watering anticipation.

Father Joe said, "I should be given a break from the pulpit more often. Would you teach me how to talk to the Boss like that?" He looked at Andrew fondly.

Peter chimed in, "How about listening to Him, like you're always tellin' me to do?" He lifted his water glass in toast to his mentor with a big grin.

There would be no booze at this table, not at breakfast or any other time. The sober ones were too grateful and their loved ones too blessed.

Miz Marymoll tapped her glass. "I got somethin' t' say t' yer Boss too. An' I'm old enough t' demand m' right t' be sayin' it." She looked over at Father Joe and nodded firmly.

"Hear, hear," chimed in Anika and Sally, raising their water glasses.

"Bow yer heads agin then. Father Gawd, I bin knowin' this good family fer most half a century. An' I wanna tell You, You didn't make no finer. I luv these people from th' bottom o' m' heart, Beloved. I thank Ye. Bless all yer beyootiful people everywhere, especially the Kennedys. Thank Ye fer the fine sober men around this family table an' fer the courage o' their wonder women, these fine children o' Gawd. A-MEN! There. Now we c'n eat right."

Somebody said "Yesssssss!" and they dug in.

Made in the USA
Middletown, DE
10 April 2022

63988348R10094